CHRISTMAS PRESENCE

PREQUEL TO THE CLAUS UNIVERSE

TONY BERTAUSKI

CLAUS UNIVERSE

Merry Christmas and happy holidays!

You've stumbled onto the prequel to the Claus Universe, a holiday science fiction adventure series. This reimagining brings new life to the holiday figures we all know and love, including the classics, some you might not be familiar with, and some brand new.

This series doesn't take the adventure lightly, nor does it shy away from the science fiction. It even ventures into fantasy land, unraveling holiday myths, legends, and stories in a way that feels plausible. How exactly does Santa Claus manage to travel the world in one night to deliver presents to every house? How do reindeer fly, and how does a snowman come to life?

When we were kids, we just accepted that it was magic. Frosty came to life with a simple hat, and Rudolph soared through the sky, no explanation needed.

What if all those mysteries could be explained with science fiction?

In this prequel, you're getting a glimpse of the adventure to come. You'll delve deeper into each character's life, their challenges, their loss and grief, their joy. And discover the Christmas spirit beneath it all.

And for those who've read this series... plenty of breadcrumbs to find.

Enjoy the adventure!

The Claus Universe
12-Book Series

Ebooks, physical and audiobooks:
BERTAUSKI.COM

1

"Sullivan, put your phone away," Mom said.

Van sighed but didn't argue. He slid the phone into the front pocket of his hoodie, his thumb lingering on the screen a moment longer than necessary. As soon as it was gone, the withdrawal kicked in. His fingers twitched, itchy and hollow, like they'd been tricked into thinking they'd never be bored again.

He flexed his hand a few times, then turned to stare out the window. The car smelled like his mom's perfume. Something floral and powdery that clung to the interior like static. Beneath it lurked the sour, earthy scent of dog slobber, stubborn and alive. Lenny sprawled across the backseat beside him, a mass of fur and panting heat, occasionally shoving his head under Van's arm for a scratch.

"Eyes on the road, hon," Mom said.

"I'm checking the address," Pete replied, steering with one hand while his thumb skimmed across his phone. The screen glowed in his lap.

Van leaned his head against the window. The glass was cold, and he welcomed the sting of it. Outside, a parade of Christmas lights blinked along the roofs of oversized houses. Some twinkled playfully, others pulsed with mechanical precision, synced to invisible music.

They all looked professionally installed, probably weeks before Thanksgiving.

A sagging snowman slouched in a front yard. Its head drooped sideways, eyes crooked and coal-smudged. A scarf hung from its neck like a noose. It hadn't snowed in days. Everything was gray and gritty.

They stopped at a red light. On the sidewalk stood a very short and very round man bundled in layers of wool. His beard was white and bushy, his face blank and unreadable. His hands were in his pockets, not moving, not texting, not doing anything. Just watching.

Van blinked. A sharp twinge of déjà vu hit his chest. Something about the man or the moment stirred a memory he couldn't grab hold of. It slipped past him like smoke.

He looked away, unsettled, and scratched Lenny behind the ears. The dog growled in gratitude, thumping his tail against the seat. Van let his eyes close for a moment, tilting his head back until it touched the headrest. He tried to think about what he wanted for Christmas.

Nothing came to mind. Nothing that made sense. Not clothes. Not tech. Not even games. He just didn't want this. Not the drive. Not the dinner. Not the expectations that came with it.

They turned off the main road and into a long, curved driveway lined with tiny white lights, wound through low hedges. A house that rose up like something from a movie set.

The place was massive. It had columns, arches, windows you could lose your reflection in. Every shrub had been sculpted. Every square inch dripped curated wealth.

"Hey, check out the lights!" Pete said. "And the landscaping. You worked on this last summer, remember?"

Pete tried. He always tried. Like he'd memorized a chapter from *How to Stepparent Without Making It Weird.* He was decent at it. Better than most.

But Van did remember. He remembered sweating through his shirt in July, hauling bags of mulch while gnats attacked his neck. He remembered the stiff odor of sod and the sting of blisters under his gloves.

The crew had called him Peep, because he barely spoke.

Still, it was the worst summer of his life. And unless something changed, next summer would be worse. More heat. More mulch. More silence.

Mom twisted in her seat. "Try to have fun tonight, hon. Meet some people."

"And remember, firm handshake. The way we practiced," Pete added.

Grip the webbing between thumb and pointer finger. Firm, not crushing. Three pumps, ending with a confident snap. Eye contact. Smile. Nice to meet you. Van remembered.

It was part of the image. The version of him they hoped would surface tonight, like a better, glossier Van who knew how to talk about school and sports and maybe even girls.

He remembered the first time Pete tried to coach him through it, all serious and awkward. It hadn't been as bad as the birds and bees conversation with Mom, though. And now, here they were. Walking into another evening full of strangers. Of expectations. Of things Van couldn't name but knew he didn't want.

A parking attendant stepped into view, waving them toward the snowed-in lawn with slow, deliberate motions. He wore a long, dark coat and a hood drawn low over his face. At first glance, Van thought he was wearing a mask, something white and blank.

Then the light shifted. Not a mask. A headlamp.

Its beam cut through the dusk, casting strange shadows that made his eyes look hollow. He gave a nod without a word, then turned and disappeared behind a hedge like a ghost with a clipboard.

There weren't many cars on the lawn. Maybe fifteen, all parked neatly like chess pieces. A parking attendant felt like overkill.

Rich people.

Van grabbed Lenny's leash from the floorboard. The dog stretched, shook off a cloud of loose fur, and sneezed against the window. Pete climbed out of the driver's seat, immediately brushing dog hair off his sweater with both hands like it was poison ivy.

"Did we have to bring Lenny?" he muttered.

"They love dogs, Pete. And they insisted. What was I supposed to say? No?"

"That was an option."

"It's just a couple of hours. There'll be plenty of time for Santa. Am I right, Van?"

Van was never sure if she was using Santa as some kind of code or if she actually meant the jolly old guy with the sleigh. His mom was like that. Firm believer in Christmas magic. Not the watered-down kind, either. The full-fat North Pole version.

He just stared at the house. His plan for the evening hadn't changed: find a quiet corner, retreat into the blue glow of his phone, and doom-scroll until his brain was numb. It was a time-honored teenage tradition. Van was a traditional guy.

Pete let out a low whistle, surveying the estate. "Do they really need this much house? I mean, come on. You seeing this? What'd you say, Masie? Why don't we get lights like that?"

"Because we don't have parties," Mom said, her eyes already locked on the towering front doors.

"Do we need a party to have nice things?"

"We don't have parties."

"I'm just sayin', wouldn't lights be nice?"

"You want lights? We'll get lights."

The conversation ender. Mom's classic move. Agree, forget, move on. It worked surprisingly well. Pete almost never followed up. And if he did, she had a way of making him feel like he was the one who'd forgotten.

Van admired it, in a weird way. She was good at her job. Whatever it was. Something in consulting, or finance, or PR. The details changed depending on who was asking.

They climbed the wide stone steps, Lenny leading the charge with his nose to the ground, tail high. He paused halfway up to inspect a rotund statue of Santa Claus nestled beside the banister. The jolly figure was grinning with his belly out, hand raised in a wave. Lenny sniffed the beard, gave it a suspicious grunt, and moved on.

The front door swung open. Everyone flinched. Lenny leapt back with a sharp bark, fur spiking a mohawk down his back. Van's grip tightened on the leash.

A figure stood in the doorway. It wore a long red scarf and a green robe that was thin, almost like velvet curtains. The robe hung open casually, revealing pale, smooth skin underneath. It was unclear whether it was a man or woman. The skin had a gray cast to it, like weathered metal. His or her feet were bare.

The figure extended a hand, palm up, holding out a dog treat. Lenny, ears perked, sniffed at the offering. After a tense second, he accepted it with one bite.

"Welcome. And Merry Christmas," the figure said, flat and even, like a rehearsed line. Its tone polite. "Please, come in. You do not need to remove your shoes."

Mom's hand went to her chest. Her mouth parted slightly. "Oh, my God," she whispered. "I can't believe it."

The figure stood motionless on the threshold. It was shaped like a person, dressed like one, even moved like one. But its face was wrong. Smooth and inhuman, it gleamed under the soft light of the entryway, like textured porcelain pulled from a kiln. No eyes. No mouth. Just the faint suggestion of features, outlined by dim flickers of internal light that glided beneath the surface like trapped fireflies.

As it spoke, its face shimmered. Subtle pulses of white and gold traced what could have been expressions.

Mom reached for the thing's hand and shook it. "You're an FS9 servant droid," she said.

"I am pleased to meet you," the android responded, as steady as its posture.

It turned to Van and extended a hand. The movement was fluid. No hesitation, no awkwardness. Van took it.

The handshake was cool. The skin, or whatever passed for skin, was smooth and pliable, like warmed plastic. Its grip was firm. Not crushing. Not limp. Perfect.

"What are you doing here?" Mom asked, stepping slightly closer.

"I am assisting the McNichols family."

Before anyone could object, it reached down and gently took Lenny's leash from Van's hand. Then it crouched, its movements eerily graceful, and rubbed behind the dog's ear with robotic precision. Lenny remained wary, but his tail betrayed him, thumping softly against the floor. The android had nailed the exact rhythm.

"Please, come inside," it said. "The weather is brisk."

Pete and Van exchanged a look. Not a panicked look. Not fear. More like disbelief compressed into a single breath. A robot was holding their dog's leash.

Their dog.

"You might want to back up," Mom said to the android. "They're not moving till you do."

The droid's faceplate pulsed with muted light, a soft ripple of greens and silvers. Still unreadable. It turned and glided smoothly inside, pausing just beyond the doorway.

"Guys, it's just a robot," Mom said, motioning them forward. "Nothing to be afraid of."

"We're not afraid," Pete said too quickly. "You afraid, Van? No, we just, you know... a little heads-up would've been great."

"I swear, I didn't know this would be here," Mom said. "And I don't see them every day, either."

"Every other day, then," Pete muttered.

Inside, the house defied expectations. From the outside, it looked like a rich person's Pinterest board. But inside, it opened up like something out of a dream. Wide rooms spilled into each other. The floors gleamed, polished to a mirror finish, reflecting the chandelier's golden light.

The air was warm and heavy with roasted meats, cinnamon, and the sharp, resinous bite of pine. A towering Christmas tree loomed in the center of the main hall, its branches glittering with a thousand tiny lights, ornaments catching the glow like jewels.

Somewhere deeper in the house, laughter and music floated through the air. Old jazz renditions of holiday songs. The kind that made everything feel like a vintage postcard.

"Peter!" boomed a voice from the hallway.

Mr. McNichols emerged like a storm front in a suit. Tall, red-cheeked, all energy all the time. He gripped Pete's hand in both of his, then slapped him on the back with a force that almost knocked him out.

"Good to see you, man!" he said, grinning. "Been too long."

Mrs. McNichols hovered just behind him. She was more restrained, smiling in that practiced way that suggested she'd already said hello to thirty people tonight. Her gown shimmered, subtle and expensive.

Their boxer trotted up, tail wagging, and met Lenny with a sniff. The two dogs checked each other out dog style and moved on.

"Sullivan?" Mr. McNichols said, letting out a hearty laugh. "When did you grow up, man?"

He extended a hand. Van stepped forward and met him with the handshake. Firm grip. Eye contact. Three pumps. Confident release.

"Mr. McNichols," Van said evenly. "Pleased to meet you, sir."

Pete beamed like a proud coach. As if handshaking was an Olympic sport and Van just medaled. McNichols gave a subtle nod, one veteran to another. Some silent agreement passed between them.

"I'll bet you're good with computers, huh?" Mr. McNichols's grin stretched wider as he turned toward Mom. "He's good, isn't he? When he finishes school, you tell him to come see me. I've got a job waiting."

Mom's smile stayed polite. "Not until college."

"Oh, please." He waved the idea away like it was smoke. "He'll learn more at Avocado in a week than he would at State in four years." He winked at Van, like they were in on some joke together. "I promise, you won't work for your mom."

Van gave the bare minimum of a smile, a quick twitch of the lips, and stared at the floor. He wanted to vanish. Crawl under the floorboards. Become one with the hardwood.

"Hey, uh," Mom said, pivoting with practiced grace, "what's the FS9 doing here?"

"We've been beta testing it for a few months now," McNichols said.

He gestured casually to the droid, which still stood motionless in the corner, its posture military-straight and perfectly neutral. The Avocado, Inc. logo was embroidered on McNichols's shirt just above the breast pocket. A tiny green fruit, sleek and minimalist. Not loud, but proud. Branding for those who considered themselves subtle geniuses.

Mom's red sweater had no logo. Just a silver snowflake pin. McNichols noticed. Van could tell.

"Is there another FS9 outside?" she asked.

That explained the attendant, Van realized. He thought about the android's build, the broad shoulders, the solid chest, the barely hidden pistons beneath the robe. The thing was kind of jacked, like a gym bro went full minimalist.

Van considered asking about that, like why the physique. Seemed an odd choice. But asking meant talking. Talking meant follow-ups. No thank you.

"One last thing before you run off," McNichols said, clapping Van lightly on the shoulder like he was handing off a football. "The FS9's kind of top secret, so no photos, all right?"

He gave Van a look that was meant to be friendly but landed somewhere closer to unblinking corporate security.

"This party is a soft launch," he continued. "Just data gathering, internal impressions. Nothing for the public. You can use your phone in the other room with the other kids. Just not out here."

Other kids.

Van's eyes drifted across the room, scanning for exits. Hallways. Hidden alcoves. Vents, if necessary. McNichols saw it as enthusiasm.

"Did you name it?" Mom asked, gesturing toward the android.

"We've been calling it Effy," McNichols said, rubbing the back of his neck. "But I don't think it'll stick."

"How about Jenks?" Pete offered.

McNichols turned, amused. "He?" he echoed. "Interesting choice, Pete."

Pete shrugged. "He's got butler vibes. The way he stands. That grayish... skin. Wait, is that skin?"

"Synthetic casing," McNichols said. He nodded toward Mom. "Masie was part of that design team, weren't you?"

Van turned to his mom, but she just smiled thinly and said nothing.

McNichols looked toward the droid. "How do you feel about the name Jenks?"

The FS9 tilted its head the slightest degree, like a curious dog. "I am here to help."

"Well, there you go," McNichols said. "Democracy in action. Anyway, don't go far. Jenks has got a little surprise planned for later."

Van barely heard him. His eyes followed the droid as it turned and gently guided Lenny and the McNichols' boxer, Jake, toward a corridor at the back of the house. From somewhere down that hallway came the distant sound of panting, barking, the clink of water bowls.

Van felt a magnetic pull in that direction. He didn't know what the other kids were like, didn't want to find out. If given the choice, he'd rather follow the droid and the dogs and spend the next two hours sniffing butts than endure whatever social torture awaited him in the "kids' room."

At least dogs were honest about their intentions.

Pete and Mrs. McNichols were deep in conversation, something about party catering and a school board meeting, their voices warm and familiar, like they'd known each other longer than Van realized. But he wasn't listening. Not even a little.

His eyes were scanning the room, calculating angles and obstacles. He needed a quiet place to disappear. Somewhere just out of sight but not suspiciously so.

There. Tucked behind a towering, absurd pile of wrapped presents, each box glossy and ribboned like it had come straight from a catalog, was a perfect alcove. The corner near the window. Low light. Shadowed. A cushioned bench sat nestled against the wall, flanked by potted poinsettias and a stack of unused coat racks. Prime real estate.

He'd have to time it right, though. Weave around the fireplace, skirt the chocolate fountain (which was dangerously close to a gaggle of sugared-up kids), and dodge two adults deep in a debate about local taxes. But if he pulled it off, he could vanish. Just long enough to scroll through his feed, pretend he wasn't here, and survive the night under the radar.

"Van, darling," Mrs. McNichols said, turning to him with that party-hostess smile, "let me show you where the other kids are. It's easy to get lost. We've got far too much house."

"I don't think that's possible," Pete said. "By the way, who did the lighting out front?"

He and Mrs. McNichols shifted seamlessly into a new conversation, already discussing fixtures and uplighting and whether smart bulbs were worth the investment.

Van stood suspended between two choices: follow her to the kids' room or make a break for it and risk becoming that weird boy who wandered off. Both were terrible. One was just slightly less terrible.

"Kids, this is Sullivan Holloway. Be nice."

Sullivan. No one called him that. Not unless he was in trouble. And *be nice*? That was code for: *Hey, kids. Don't judge him out loud. And not to his face.*

No one looked up. Not one person.

They were sunken into oversized bean bags, glowing from below like aliens around a campfire, every single one of them lit by the cold, flickering light of their phones. The room was a recreational paradise with pinball machines humming in standby, a ping pong table untouched, air hockey with abandoned paddles, and a trampoline. Yeah, a trampoline. There was even a vintage arcade lineup of *Galaga*, *Street Fighter II*, and a racing game with actual motorcycles to ride.

And yet, no one moved.

Van hovered awkwardly in the doorway until Pete gave his arm a quick squeeze. Not a push. Not a shove. Just a silent *good luck, buddy*, like he was dropping Van off at summer camp. Then, right before he left, he pointed toward the group of girls and mouthed something Van didn't want to decipher.

Heat rushed to his face. Full-on combustion. His ears went hot. His cheeks burned. He could feel sweat prickling under his arms, his heart giving one hard kick in his chest. For a second, he thought he might actually pass out.

He stayed in the doorway, pretending to be interested in the massive garage-door television screen on the wall. It was playing *It's a Wonderful Life*, which was both ironic and cruel. He wasn't planning to stay. Just long enough to look like he tried. Then he'd find a hallway closet and wait the night out in blissful darkness.

He knew who was in the room. Even if they didn't know him. Student government royalty. Honor society lifers. Debate team kids who actually liked debating. Their photos filled the yearbook like campaign posters. If you asked Van, he'd say he didn't know their names.

He did. He knew *all* their names. Especially Charli.

Charlotte Marie McNichols was her name. It felt like a lyric. It played on loop in his head some days. Her favorite color was green. Not forest green or lime green. Just green. She loved kale salads (yes, *loved*) with fake bacon bits and thousand island dressing. Her spirit animal was a tabby cat, according to a quiz she once took. She chewed her fingernails but hated that she did.

Van could tell you which days she wore her ponytail with a simple black elastic and which days she went with the fancy French braid that meant she had a presentation or something important. Her hair was the color of maple leaves in October, but somehow, she smelled like summer. Like mango body spray and sunscreen and open windows.

Watching her walk back from communion was the only reason he wanted to go to church.

Right now, her face glowed in the dim room, lit by her phone. Her brow furrowed slightly, concentrating on something. Maybe a text, maybe a meme. Van stared like she was a fire in the middle of a frozen field.

If any of the others looked up, they might laugh. They might scream. He was staring like she was famous. Or food.

He hadn't expected her to be here. She lived here, sure. But people like her always had better places to be.

She didn't belong in the kids' room with the rest of them. She should've been at some exclusive thing, sipping something with pomegranate seeds while laughing under a canopy of mistletoe. Not sunk into a bean bag in her own house like a mortal.

And yet here she was. Van knew he should look away, but he was lost in a daydream.

In it, Charli would tell everyone to leave. She'd stand up, point to the door, and everyone would groan and shuffle off. But not him. She'd tell Van to stay. And it wouldn't be weird. They'd just sit there in the soft crater of the beanbags, not talking, just swiping through their phones side by side. Occasionally, she'd show him something funny. He'd help her beat a level in whatever game she was playing. Her hand would brush his. Eventually, she'd rest her chin on his shoulder to watch him tap the screen.

He could feel the weight of that moment, the way her breath would warm the side of his neck and—

"Aren't you in history?"

Van flinched so hard he almost made a noise. For a second, he thought maybe Charli was talking to someone else, someone behind him, but when she looked up, their eyes met. Just for a second. But it was enough to send his heart through the roof, past the attic, into the sky, where it disintegrated somewhere above the moon.

He opened his mouth, but his brain was stuck in neutral. Before he could shape a single word, Jace spoke.

"Adams knows more about cars than history," he muttered without looking up.

Jace sat cross-legged in a beanbag, wearing a long-sleeve mesh shirt under a ripped tank. His bleach-blond hair dipped in black at the ends gave him the look of a rebellious candle. His ears were a constellation of studs and rings, catching the flicker of TV light.

Van and Jace had never spoken, even though they both sat near the back of history class. It was true Mr. Adams loved cars. Talked about them constantly. More than the Civil War. More than the Constitution. At one point, Van was pretty sure Adams had compared Jefferson to a V8 engine.

But no one acknowledged the comment. The room remained glued to its screens, each person basking in their own private orbit of LED-blue solitude.

Van shifted his weight. Too late now to answer Charli. The moment had passed, and he'd missed it completely.

Sera, tallest of the group and queen of indifference, lounged sideways on a beanbag that looked like it was melting around her. Her T-shirt was oversized enough to be a dress, sleeves swallowing her hands. The rips in her jeans looked earned, not purchased, and she wore them like armor.

She leaned over and showed Charli something on her phone. Whatever it was earned a grin, followed by a burst of laughter that came from somewhere deep. Van felt a stab of envy. Then Charli handed her phone to Sera.

"What happened?" Sera asked, squinting at the screen.

"He said someone put a nail in his tire," Charli replied, brushing a strand of hair behind her ear.

Sera made a face. "Wait, that's why he's not here? A flat tire?"

Charli shrugged. The kind of shrug that could mean anything. Or nothing. Her lips twisted slightly. Maybe amused. Maybe annoyed.

They were talking about Bobby. Not her boyfriend. Not officially. But he was always there. Waiting after school. Holding her books. Sitting beside her at lunch. Laughing too loud. Staring too long.

He drove a new truck, charcoal gray, with speakers loud enough to rattle lockers when he pulled into the parking lot. His family didn't have McNichols-level wealth, but they were in the upper brackets.

"Wait," Marla said, lifting her head. "How does he know someone put a nail in it?"

Marla's voice always had an edge to it, like she'd just solved a puzzle you didn't know existed. Her dark curls were half-pinned, half-loose, like she couldn't decide on a mood. She squinted at the screen, leaning toward Charli.

"Someone saw someone doing something to it," Charli said vaguely. "I don't know."

"*Someone* saw *someone*," Marla repeated. "Makes sense."

Charli sighed. "He had to buy a new tire."

And just like that, the moment dissolved. The thread snipped. Everyone slid back into the embrace of their phones. The laughter was gone. Just the click and flick of scrolling fingers filled the room now.

Van reached for his phone. It had been in his pocket the whole time, untouched. He pulled it out, just to give his hands something to do. He wasn't even going to look at anything specific. Just something bright. Something numbing.

But then he heard it. The click. The sharp, precise cadence of heels on hardwood. Walking with purpose.

"What time is it?" Charli asked.

Sera glanced at her phone and answered with a single word.

Charli sprang up from the beanbag like she'd been jolted with electricity. She moved faster than anyone expected, scrambled beneath the air hockey table in one fluid motion. Her hair fanned out behind her, catching the light as she ducked, her body curling into the shadows.

They could all still see her, though. Her head poked out from under the table like a startled cat, eyes wide, lips pressed tight.

Without hesitation, Erica began stacking couch cushions in front of the table like sandbags before a storm. It was an obvious barricade. Anyone looking would know someone was hiding. But that didn't matter. It wasn't about being invisible. Plausible deniability.

Mrs. McNichols didn't come close enough to the room to notice anyway.

"Sullivan?" she called down the hallway. "Would you tell the kids it's time?"

Van blinked. *Time?*

His eyes swept across the room, then back toward the hallway.

She didn't stick around for a reply. Her heels tapped a retreating rhythm, fading into the distance like a metronome winding down.

"She leave?" Charli whispered from her hiding place.

Marla army-crawled to the doorway and leaned just far enough to peek. "She's gone," she confirmed.

"Good. If she asks," Charli said, "tell her I'm in the bathroom."

A quiet agreement passed through the room like a shared spell. A contract of silence. No one questioned it.

One by one, they stood and stretched, brushing crumbs off their shirts and stuffing phones into pockets. They drifted toward the hallway, casual but coordinated, like birds lifting from a power line all at once.

Sera was the last to go. When she noticed Van lingering, still rooted by indecision, she grabbed his sleeve and gave it a tug.

"Come on."

He hesitated. "Is Charli coming?"

Sera leaned in, close enough that he could smell spearmint gum. "Didn't you hear?" she said, with a wink. "She's in the bathroom."

Everyone had gathered in the great room now, forming a loose semicircle around the fireplace. Conversation buzzed like static, the air charged with a kind of expectant wonder. It felt like Christmas Eve, like something magical might happen if you waited long enough.

At the center of the room, the FS9 droid stood on a chair. Even elevated, it held perfect balance, its posture straight and composed, towering above the crowd like a digital angel atop a tree.

The lighting was soft and golden. Firelight danced across the polished floor. There was laughter and murmurs, but underneath it all was a silence that came with anticipation. It felt like Santa Claus was about to slide down the chimney.

Across the room, Mom spotted Van. She smiled, eyes lighting up when she saw him standing beside Sera and the others. She gave a little wave. For once, Van didn't feel like he was on the outside looking in. He wasn't lurking in a corner or hiding behind furniture. He was part of something. That's what she saw.

What she didn't know was why he was still there. Why he hadn't disappeared to a bathroom or a closet or a coat rack. Why he hadn't ghosted the night like he always did.

It wasn't the droid. It wasn't the holiday magic. It was Charli.

And Charli was hiding. *Didn't you hear?*

A second droid entered the room, the one from the parking lot. Its long coat was gone, revealing dull gray skinwrap over muscled arms. Behind it came the dogs.

Lenny pushed to the front immediately, tail wagging like a caffeinated metronome. He ignored the people. He ignored the droid. He made a straight line to Van and parked himself at his feet.

People turned. Laughed. Reached down to pet the star of the party. Van felt the glow of that attention settle on him. He didn't deserve it, but he let it happen. Sometimes, proximity was enough.

"Where's Charli?" Mrs. McNichols asked, scanning the room.

"She's in the bathroom," Erica said without looking up from her phone.

Mrs. McNichols frowned. Just for a second. Concern flitted across her face, quick and subtle. She looked like she might go check, but then something caught her attention.

A murmur rippled through the crowd. People were pointing.

The FS9's faceplate, once smooth and blank, now showed an image like a television screen. A face. Not realistic. Not exactly. More like an old animation.

The face had sharp features, a pinched brow, and spectacles. It looked like something out of a storybook. A familiar sneer curled its digital lips.

"Merry Christmas, Mr. Scrooge!" someone called out.

And the room erupted in laughter. Even Van smiled. But in the back of his mind, he couldn't stop thinking about the girl under the air hockey table. Hiding. From something.

Or someone. Or maybe everything.

The droid's gray hand lifted in an awkward, half-hearted wave. It was jarring. His posture, once statuesque, had slumped slightly. The movement was stiff. Mechanical, yes, but also tired. Like a weary politician, smiling through another handshake he didn't want to give. He raised his hand again, this time slower, lazier, as though unsure if anyone was still watching.

"Merry, merry, all," he grumbled, flat and joyless, like someone reciting lines from a long-forgotten play.

There was applause. Scattered. Uncertain.

Mr. McNichols stepped up with gusto, shaking the droid's hand like an old celebrity just finished an oldie but goodie. The projected face of Ebenezer Scrooge flashed another forced grin and wished the room a hearty *Merry Christmas!* in a tone that couldn't have sounded more disinterested. The smile never reached his eyes.

The whole thing felt rehearsed, like a tech demo. And yet, the room responded like it was real theater. Smiles. Nods. Another wave of polite, sluggish applause. Then, just like that, Ebenezer Scrooge tapped out.

The faceplate returned to its original blank grayness. No eyes. No expression. Just a reflective surface that caught the firelight and threw it back cold.

The droid stepped down from the chair with mechanical care, landing heavier than expected. The applause fizzled into silence.

"What was that?" Sera whispered.

"Charli's dad showing off the robot," Erica replied, unimpressed.

"With the weird face on it?"

"I think it was so everyone could kiss the boss," Jace said. "Why else would they clap?"

No one had a better theory.

Weirdness hung in the air like glitter that wouldn't fall. A robot had stood on a chair and said *Merry Christmas* with a projected frown, and everyone had clapped like it was normal.

The others were already drifting back toward the game room. Sera glanced back at Van. Their eyes met, and hers widened slightly. Coming?

He felt it again. The heat in his cheeks, the surge of being seen. And without even thinking, he followed.

"Did you get it?" Erica whispered.

Charli wasn't in the bathroom. She wasn't under the air hockey table. She was on Beanbag Mountain. Perched like a queen in a throne of vinyl, her eyes gleaming with mischief. She waved them over urgently, gesturing with both hands.

Van was the last one in. He closed the door quietly, half expecting someone to shout or burst in behind them.

Charli tossed a beanbag toward the door. Then another. Then another.

Sera and Marla helped, laughing under their breath. They stacked the cushions high, a ridiculous barricade that would stop no one.

Charli held a small black box in her lap. It was sleek and rectangular, perfectly square at the corners, lined with soft edges and a subtle shimmer. It didn't look like a gift. It looked like something that belonged in a vault.

She opened it slowly. Inside, nestled in crushed velvet, were two pairs of sunglasses. They weren't normal sunglasses. These were sculpted, futuristic. One pair had a greenish tint, like reflective emerald. The other looked almost like translucent obsidian.

They looked like something out of a fashion week video. Or a spy movie. Or both.

Charli's dad brought home things from work. Prototypes, designs, test models. Things that weren't supposed to leave the office or the closet in the back of his walk-in wardrobe. But Charli knew about that closet.

Snooping is a skill, she once said in class.

Some kids played sports. Charli hunted secrets. And she was good at it. Now she was holding one.

"Did you try them on?" Marla asked, leaning closer.

"Not yet," Charli said.

"Yeah, I don't get it." Jace picked up one of the pairs. "They're ugly."

"They're not for the sun, idiot," Erica snapped, snatching them out of his hand.

So apparently, they weren't sunglasses. Van felt his brain click into a different gear.

Charli had found them a few weeks ago, tucked in the farthest, most off-limits corner of her dad's closet. Not with the Christmas presents. Not in the usual Avocado product bins. These were separate. Hidden. That had to mean something.

If they were just fashion prototypes or weird luxury wearables, he doubted her dad would have bothered to bury them behind a row of travel suits.

Charli handed one of the pairs to Marla, who cradled it in her hands like a science artifact. She turned it over, inspecting every angle. The frame was clean and futuristic. Minimalist in a way that seemed expensive. The lenses were big and flat, tinted dark enough to absorb light. The arms were blocky, thick near the hinge, with an embedded silver band that curved around to the back.

They looked like the kind of thing your grandfather would wear over his real glasses on a bright day.

How many people could pull those off? No one in this room. But what did Van know about fashion. He only wore one brand of T-shirt.

"So, what do we do with them?" Marla asked.

"Put them on," Charli said.

"And then what?"

Charli shrugged. "I don't know. I heard my dad say something about highwire gaming. They look like goggles, right?"

"Goggles?" Sera raised an eyebrow. "I mean, for boomers, maybe."

Marla tapped the side of the band where two small temple pads were embedded. "What are these?"

"Like I know?" Charli replied, holding up her own pair.

"You know more than us. Are you seriously going to put something on your face when you have no idea what it does?" Marla said.

"I'll do it." The words slipped out of Van's mouth before he could pull them back.

Everyone turned. Like they'd forgotten he was even there.

Van didn't shrink from it. Not this time. He'd spent years escaping into screens, hundreds of hours immersed in games, simulations, stories built from code and sound and light. If this was anything like a new gaming platform, he was probably the most qualified person in the room.

Charli snatched the glasses from Marla. "Come on, Sullivan. You and me."

There was a murmur of back-and-forth from the others. Jace muttered something under his breath. Marla looked mildly wounded but also visibly relieved. Being first came with risk, and no one wanted to be the guinea pig.

They shifted positions, forming a loose semicircle. A spotlight of silence fell on Van as he crossed his legs and settled into place beside Charli.

"It's Van," he said quietly.

"I know," Charli replied.

She handed him the second pair. They felt cool and solid in his hands. The metal band glided over his skin like melted ice. No buttons. No switches. No ports for charging. Just smooth, matte black lenses so dark they absorbed the room.

Inside the band, almost invisible, was a tiny line of etched silver. *Christmas Presence.*

It was barely there. The kind of detail meant for the person wearing them.

"Ready?" Charli asked.

Van looked up. Their eyes locked. She smiled.

And just like that, the butterflies in his stomach were activated, flapping hard enough to lift him off the floor.

Charli raised her glasses like a toast. He mirrored her, their hands almost touching. The moment pulsed with something electric, a silent dare. Together, they slid them on.

The effect was instant.

THE WEIGHT SETTLED around his head, heavier than expected. Not uncomfortable, but noticeable. It was like placing a helmet over his senses. The lenses swallowed his vision completely. Not even a hint of peripheral light. Just black.

Not like closing your eyes. Worse. A total erasure. No shapes. No shadows. No glow. Just absence.

Then the pads at his temples warmed. Slowly. Then faster. A pulsing rhythm began, one that didn't match his heart rate. It was faster, more urgent. Pressure built behind his eyes.

He reached up instinctively, fingers twitching near the frames. He wanted to take them off.

Instead, he turned his head slightly, just enough to sense motion beside him, to confirm Charli was still there. He wanted to ask if she felt it too. But his mouth wouldn't move.

Something had begun. Something neither of them could see.

"What's going on?"

Erica's voice reached them like it was traveling through water. Van tried to focus on it, to hold onto the sound, but it slipped away like two trains speeding in opposite directions.

His heart was racing, slamming against his ribs in sync with the pulses at his temples. The pressure was climbing, rising like a storm tide. Then came the drop. Not metaphorical. The floor beneath him vanished.

He was falling.

No wind. No movement in his limbs. Just the nauseating pull of gravity dragging his stomach into his throat. A pure elevator-plunge sensation that stole his breath. He nearly tore the glasses off. But something deep inside, some primal flicker of instinct or trust or stubborn curiosity told him to hang on.

Don't move. Just wait.

And then a pinpoint shimmer in the void. It glimmered faintly, like the first star on a winter night. Then it bloomed, morphing, unfolding in impossible colors. It poured into the blackness like spilled paint across a canvas, cascading in every direction.

Within seconds, the darkness was gone. A floor appeared beneath his feet. Solid, smooth. A ceiling emerged above. The world constructed itself around him like a simulation booting up in real time.

Van turned slowly. This wasn't the game room. This wasn't any room he knew.

And across from him, sitting cross-legged on the glowing floor, was Charli. It wasn't a hologram. Not a cartoon. Not an avatar. It was her. Charli. The real one. Every freckle, every strand of hair, every flicker of breath. She was there, physically there with him.

Her face was somewhere between awe and panic, her eyes wide, unblinking. She looked around in disbelief, then met his gaze.

"Whoooooa," she breathed.

They both turned slowly, taking it in. The space stretched in every direction, wider than it should've been, deeper than it seemed. Colors shifted with the light, bending reality into soft, impossible shapes.

The walls weren't walls. They moved slightly, like glass that breathed.

"What is it?" Marla's voice filtered in, still distant, still echoing.

Charli's fingers brushed his. Then her hand wrapped around his. A pulse of warmth shot through him, chasing out every doubt. Charli's grip was gentle but unwavering. She pulled him to his feet with practiced ease.

He stood. He didn't let go. He didn't want to let go.

For a moment, the space around them faded into background noise. It didn't matter what this place was or how it worked. She was holding his hand, and everything felt weightless. Perfect. Like this world existed just for them.

Best Christmas ever didn't even come close.

"IT'S A LOBBY," Van said, after they had explored a little. "Like a starting point."

He knew the feel of it. The layout. It was familiar, but not cliché. A place where players chose their missions, sorted their gear, or waited for the next level to load. A kind of digital purgatory with clean lines and ambient lighting.

The walls were lined with blank monitors. A massive wraparound control panel curved in front of them, like a futuristic cockpit. Rows of buttons, keys, and glowing icons stretched across the surface.

But there were no prompts. No menus. No instructions.

Van reached out and grabbed a joystick. It moved. He flinched and yanked his hand back.

"What happened?" Sera asked. Her voice echoed from wherever the outside world still touched this one.

"I didn't expect to, uh…" Van shook his hand. "To feel it."

"Feel what?"

Van glanced down at the panel again. "The feedback. The resistance. It wasn't virtual. It felt like… like I was touching something."

He looked up at Charli, who was already moving toward another station, eyes scanning the unfamiliar interface.

"This isn't a game," Van said. "It's something else."

Charli nodded, slow and deliberate. A grin started to form at the corners of her mouth—curiosity and awe battling for control.

Then, one of the monitors flickered.

The room, until now dormant and inert, seemed to inhale.

A blinking red cursor appeared at the top of the screen.

A message began to type itself.

WELCOME, PLAYER ONE.

WELCOME, PLAYER TWO.

Van's pulse jumped. He could hear it, could feel it in his ears, a drumbeat building behind his eyes.

The screen flashed again.

PLEASE SELECT A DOOR.

Without warning, the floor lit up in front of them. Three glowing doors rose from nothing.

They shimmered faintly, casting soft light across the walls. Each one looked solid and unreal at the same time. Like a dream pretending to be architecture. They didn't hum or whir or open. They just stood. Waiting.

Van opened his mouth to say something but stopped himself.

He tried again to explain the joystick, the cool press of plastic against his fingertips. How it had texture, the subtle give of it. How that moment had made him question whether he was still sitting in a beanbag back on Earth, or if he had stepped into something else entirely.

But the words didn't carry the weight of the experience. The magic of it slipped through translation.

The immersion wasn't just visual or tactile. It was emotional. Spatial. Like the air in here pressed differently against his skin. Like the world had rules, but none he'd seen before.

They kept walking the perimeter of the lobby. Not moving fast. Still trying to figure it out.

The walls were unremarkable. Panels and flickering lights, like a control room without an operator. The grayed-out monitors stayed stubbornly blank, no matter what Charli did. She pressed buttons. Pulled levers. Nothing changed.

Marla's voice echoed in from somewhere distant. "Can I get a turn?"

Van was about to say yes. A cold realization slid into his chest. He didn't know how to *leave*.

He lifted his hand to his face, touching his cheek, then his forehead. There were no glasses on his face. And yet the warm pads against his temples pulsed steadily. The only clue they were still there. If not for that sensation, he might've believed he'd taken them off already.

His fingers paused against his skin. Was this even his face anymore?

He turned to Charli, about to ask her to pull the glasses off him, just to make sure he was still himself, when she started walking toward one of the doors. She was heading for the middle one. The red one. It stood like a heartbeat in the center of the room, glowing softly. The color of warning signs. Of stoplights.

Van had logged a lot of hours in video games. A lot, a lot. He'd built empires, fought monsters, solved puzzles that bent logic in half. There were moments in games when the smartest strategy wasn't thinking. It was just doing. You opened the mysterious chest. You walked down the corridor. You clicked yes. Sometimes, you had to find out what happened.

This wasn't one of those times.

Video games had rules. You could pause. You could quit. You could respawn. If things went south, you turned off the console and went to grab a snack. Watched TV. Walked the dog.

This felt real. Too real.

The air had weight. The space had flavor. Like electricity, like metal. The tension in his legs, the tightness in his chest was his body responding like this was life, not code. Now was not the time to throw open a glowing red door and hope a dozen aliens didn't spill out holding laser cannons and bad attitudes.

If it had been anyone else, he would've said something. Warned them. Stopped them. But it was Charli.

She stepped up to the door and placed her hand on the handle. Red light bled from the edges. Soft and pulsing, like the glow of a sleeping ember. From somewhere beyond, he heard the sound of sleigh bells. Distant Christmas music, warped slightly by space or time, echoed faintly through the crack. It sounded innocent.

That was the problem.

Charli looked back at him. She smiled. And that smile hit Van like a warm gust in winter.

She didn't step forward. Didn't open it. Didn't move at all.

Van shifted just enough to get a better angle, to see what she was looking at. And then it happened.

Charli was sucked into the light. Like the door inhaled and pulled her into it. One second she was there, the next she was gone. Van's stomach dropped through the floor.

"No!"

He lunged forward. His hand stretched out blindly. And some-how, miraculously, his fingers caught hers. They latched together.

She didn't scream, but he felt it in the tension of her grip. The panic. And then the light fell on him, too.

Everything warped. Sound vanished in an instant, like someone had flipped the world's mute button. The game room. The beanbags. The voices of her friends.

Gone.

THEY WERE GREETED BY SILENCE. And a panda.

It stood at the edge of a narrow aisle, like a stuffed sentry, gently nodding in time with the red balloon tied to its arm. The balloon swayed in slow motion, as if underwater. The panda's green button eyes reflected the low ambient light. One was scratched. Its fur was matted. But it felt alive, somehow. Present.

The space beyond could only loosely be called a workshop.

In truth, it felt more like a forgotten wing of some interdimensional thrift store. A treasure trove of toys, trinkets, and oddities stretched from floor to ceiling in precarious towers. There were wind-up animals with chipped paint, glass globes that glowed faintly from within, and shelves of mechanical arms and puppet heads with blinking eyes.

The room was dense with forgotten magic. Each aisle was barely wide enough for two people to walk shoulder to shoulder. It felt like a labyrinth, constructed from imagination and memory.

The panda, still waving, stood watch at the threshold, its red balloon brushing gently against the ceiling.

Van and Charli didn't speak. Their mouths slightly open, breath visible in the icy air. The cold nipped at their cheeks and fingers. The world around them was too much and not enough, all at once.

The clarity was unsettling. Hyperreal. Like putting on glasses after years of blurry vision and realizing the world had edges you'd never noticed before.

Without meaning to, the backs of their hands brushed again. This time, Van didn't pull away. Neither did she.

"What is this?" he whispered.

Charli shook her head, her expression unreadable.

Van had been expecting the next level of a video game. This, though. This was something else entirely. He blinked hard, trying to pull his brain back into focus. The air smelled like frost and peppermint.

He stepped forward into a narrow aisle and immediately slipped. The floor wasn't just slick. It was ice. Frozen solid, as smooth and unforgiving as a hockey rink. Charli grabbed the back of his shirt to steady him. He mumbled a quick "Thanks," still looking down, too distracted to meet her gaze.

The ceiling curved low and narrow, forcing him into a hunch. Frost crept along the edges in delicate spirals, like frozen vines. Every step was careful, deliberate, their breath puffing clouds into the air. It was like sneaking through a forgotten ice tunnel carved into the spine of a mountain.

Then the space opened up. It wasn't a hallway. It was some kind of workshop or storeroom. But chaos ruled here. Boxes had spilled their contents across the icy floor in a strange, surreal avalanche. Umbrellas, feathers, wooden canes with polished handles. Nothing made sense. Yet somehow, it all belonged. Like a dream pretending to be a garage sale.

They turned a corner. A long workbench stood against the far wall, its surface cluttered with pieces of projects mid-creation. The shelves above overflowed with crates, burlap sacks, and mismatched bins. Wires. Gears. Springs. Doll arms made of plastic and rubber. Strings of blinking lights that flickered in no particular rhythm. A row of plastic eyes stared out from a jar.

Above the bench, a collage of drawings blanketed the wall. Blueprints and schematics, hand-drawn and annotated. Designs of stuffed animals and mechanical toys. Teddy bears with hinged arms. Pandas with wind-up keys. Dragons with gear-driven wings.

At the far end of the bench, a red coat hung from the back of a small wooden chair. It looked soft but heavy. Dusty. Weathered, but not abandoned. The kind of coat someone lived in.

Van took a few steps closer, eyes scanning the mess. Rivets, nails, coils of string. Bottles of glue. Half-assembled dolls with glassy, too-human eyes. A row of toy cars, some pristine, others with their wheels snapped off. It was a museum of half-finished joy.

And then there was the gingerbread man.

He was leaning against the wall like he belonged there. It looked handmade, with frosted buttons and cinnamon-speckled edges. He picked it up. The scent of nutmeg was strong. He didn't even think. He bit into it.

"Can you taste it?" Charli asked.

Van nodded, chewing slowly. "Yeah. It's… it's sweet. Like… really sweet."

"Too sweet?" she asked.

"Like sugar on top of sugar," he replied, licking a crumb from his lip.

Charli took the gingerbread man when he offered it, studying it with a curious tilt of her head. The light from above made her face glow. There was something animated about her now. Like she had been touched up, enhanced, as if this place had subtly dialed her into some dreamlike version of herself.

Van turned away. If he looked at her a second longer, she might read him like a screen. Might see every unspoken thought flickering across his face with subtitles.

What is this place?

There was no mission. No tutorial. No map in the corner. No pause menu. Just an immersive space that felt too real to be artificial, too fantastical to be real. It didn't feel like VR. It felt like stepping into someone else's imagination.

He drifted further into the cluttered maze, brushing his fingers over cold metal, smooth glass, and frayed bits of cloth. Each surface told its own story. There was no goal. No prize. For the first time in a long time, Van felt something like joy. Just being there. Just being.

Then he saw the hat. And everything changed.

AT FIRST, it was just another oddity in the clutter. A floppy green hat with a tiny golden bell stitched to the tip. Van barely glanced at it. But then the cold pinched at his ears, and something tugged at the edge of his thoughts. The hat looked warm. Inviting. Cozy in a way nothing else in this icy maze had.

Without thinking, he picked it up. *Ring-a-ding.*

The bell chimed, soft but sharp, a crystalline note that sliced the air like a blade. And the room reacted.

The walls shuddered. Dust fell from the ceiling in sudden flurries. The air thickened around them, charged like the moment before a lightning strike.

"What's happening?" Charli said.

"I—I don't know."

Overhead, the string lights flashed in frantic bursts, each flicker throwing their shadows across the chaos in broken, twitching silhouettes. Then the siren started. An alarm that screamed in jagged pulses, stabbing Van's skull with every blast.

He winced and grabbed at his face, instinctively trying to pull off the glasses. But there was nothing there. No edges. No seams. No pressure against the bridge of his nose.

Like the glasses had never existed. Like this was his body now.

"Charli, come on!"

He seized her wrist and yanked her into the labyrinth of clutter, dodging between teetering stacks of forgotten artifacts. She kept close, one hand on the back of his shirt, bunching it up between his shoulders as they moved. Fast. Half-running, half-skidding. A blur of motion in a world losing its mind.

The debris blurred into madness. Umbrellas, doll parts, bundles of wires, old typewriters. It all smeared together as they raced, trying to find the path back. Van's breath burned in his lungs. His heart jackhammered in his chest.

Then he stopped. The landmarks were wrong.

They had passed the umbrella cans. The box of canes. But now nothing matched. No familiar crates. No scattered drawings. Instead, there were tubs of feathers, scrolls tied with ribbon, mechanical birds with shattered wings.

"Wait," he whispered.

Charli glanced around. "Are we trapped?"

Before he could answer, he heard it. A sound that wasn't there before.

There, just beyond the workbench. A whisper of movement. The faint slooshing of something sliding across the icy floor. The air went colder.

So, the game begins.

That thought was a jolt. This wasn't random. They were being hunted. Surrounded. He couldn't see them, but he could feel them pressing in, boxing them inside the maze of aisles. His hand clenched around the green hat.

Ring-a-ding. The bell rang again, shrill and mocking. And everything went dead quiet.

Van's stomach dropped. The silence was worse than the sirens.

Without thinking, he jammed the hat deep into the pocket of his cargo pants, muffling the bell with shaking hands. He turned, searching frantically. They needed a distraction. Anything.

Then he saw it.

One aisle over, near the ceiling. The red balloon.

He leaned into a tall rack of metal trays and gear parts and shoved with all his weight. The entire structure swayed, then toppled. Plates shattered. Tin pans rang out like gunshots. A cacophony of crashes surged through the space like thunder.

He grabbed Charli and pulled her through the chaos.

He sprinted past the panda with green button eyes. A single red balloon tied to its stubby arm, twisting lazily as if waiting for this exact moment.

The red door was there. It was open. He dove through it.

Charli was right behind him.

THE WAY out was a corridor of sleepy nowhereness. Of soft edges and quiet air. Time unraveling at the seams.

Then came the sniffing.

Van stirred. His arms felt like sandbags. He fumbled upward and brushed against the blackout glasses clinging to his face. He knocked them off. Lenny was there, tail wagging, nose inspecting the frames. Across from him, Jake was happily licking Charli's cheek while she sat on the floor, unmoving.

Weren't we standing?

They had been. He remembered that clearly. Charli had taken his hand. That moment was solid in his memory, sharp and vivid. But now they were seated again, the lights were back on, and the magic was gone.

Sera moved quickly, scooping up the glasses before anyone else could notice. She slid them into the black case and shoved it beneath a nearby beanbag just as a head appeared in the doorway.

"Having fun, are we?" Pete asked with a grin.

Van's mom was there, too, beaming like she'd just walked in on her son scoring the winning goal. He was making friends. Real ones. Not the virtual kind. Not avatars on message boards or usernames in chat threads. Actual kids. In the actual world.

A few other adults from the tour group trailed in behind her, pausing to marvel at the size of the game room. They commented on the pinball machine, the projector screen, the candy-colored beanbags.

No one noticed Charli's blank stare.

Van's senses were still crawling back. As if his brain had to climb out of a deep well. He blinked rapidly. The toy workshop didn't feel virtual. Not the way video games did. It had weight. Texture.

"Time to go," his mom said gently. "Come on, Len."

The dog trotted over without protest.

Charli's friends looked at one another. Something silent passed between them. Then Sera stepped forward with casual confidence.

"Van can stay, if it's all right. We're doing a sleepover."

Van's heart kicked.

His mom raised an eyebrow. "This close to Christmas?"

"Uh, yeah," Sera said. "It's no big deal. We do it all the time."

Her tone was breezy, but there was tension beneath it. A wire pulled too tight. Van's mom looked to Charli for confirmation.

"Your parents are okay with this?"

Charli didn't answer right away. Sera gave her a tiny nudge.

"Yeah. Yeah." Charli rubbed her face like she was trying to wake herself up. "We do it all the time."

For a second, Van thought it might actually work. That his mom might say yes.

But he saw the shift in her expression. The narrowing of her eyes. The quick glance at Charli, taking in her pale face, the disoriented look, the way her hands fidgeted with nothing at all.

"Not tonight, dear."

It sounded like a closed door.

Van stood on unsteady legs, knees wobbling beneath him like he'd just learned to walk. His mom already had Lenny's leash in hand and was heading out.

On the drive home, she would ask why he was walking so funny. He'd mumble something about sitting too long. His legs had fallen asleep. She wouldn't buy it. Not with the way Charli had looked. Not with the weird, quiet tension in that room.

Later, she'd say something about how strange the whole thing was. About how maybe these weren't the kind of friends she wanted him to have.

He waved goodbye, thinking he'd probably never talk to Charli again. He was wrong about that.

He was wrong about a lot of things.

2

Something was at Van's bedroom door.

He didn't move. Just listened. Then came the snuffling.

If he were ten, he'd already know what it was. No question. It was a monster. The kind that crept up the stairs after midnight and stood outside your room, waiting. A knuckle-dragging shadow with yellow eyes and claws that tapped the wood floor.

But Van was seventeen. He didn't believe in monsters. He didn't believe in much of anything. Still, he stayed frozen under the covers, as if being very still might make the world go still, too.

Then came a high-pitched whine. A low, questioning *woof.*

Van let out a breath, relieved and annoyed all at once. He shoved the blankets off and sat up. Still wearing the same clothes from the Christmas party. Not unusual. He crossed the room and opened the door.

Lenny barreled in, all tail and tongue. The big dog swept the carpet like he was tracking invisible crumbs. Van dragged a hand through his messy hair and padded to the bathroom.

When he came back, Lenny wasn't sniffing anymore. He was staring at the closet. Still as a statue.

Now, if a ten-year-old knew anything, it was this: monsters didn't live under beds. That was for dust bunnies, missing socks, and the occasional pizza crust. The closet? That's where the real nightmares lived.

Normally, Van wouldn't even flinch at a closed door. But it was three in the morning. If it weren't for the dog, he'd have done the smart thing and crawled back into bed. Maybe pulled the covers over his head, just for old times' sake.

Instead, he opened the closet. And stepped back.

Lenny dove in nose-first, rustling through a pile of clothes. Van watched, his pulse ticking a little faster. The dog sniffed, circled, nosed deeper. But nothing jumped out. No troll. No goblin. No secret passage to a frozen toy workshop.

Just clothes.

Van exhaled and reached for the door. That's when his foot brushed something soft. He looked down. A sweatshirt. It was damp. He crouched, frowning, and ran his fingers over the fabric.

The rest of the clothes beneath it were soaked and cold, like they'd been left out in the rain. Or worse, buried in snow.

Half the closet floor was a mess of clothes, more than usual, most of them not on hangers. He hadn't done this. At least... he didn't think he had.

Lenny gave himself a shake and trotted over to his dog bed, circling once before collapsing in a heap.

Van stared at the sweatshirt.

Maybe Pete had let Lenny out earlier, and he came in with wet paws. Maybe the clothes had fallen.

No.

Because the sweatshirt had snow on it.

VAN'S PHONE buzzed against his leg.

Gray light leaked through the frost-rimmed window. He stirred, groggy, fumbling for it. It was still in the front pocket of his cargo pants. He yanked it free just as it buzzed again. He blinked away the sleep and read the screen.

Call me.

That wasn't what made him sit up straight. It was the name above the message.

He rubbed his eyes, blinked, squinted. Read it again.

Charli.

When did I put her in my phone? More importantly... why would she text me?

There was another text, sent at 3:31 a.m. Same message.

This had to be a joke. One of her friends. Jace, probably. He'd never liked Van. It was just a setup, some prank to get him to call her and wake her up and make a fool of himself. That had to be it. Why else would she reach out?

Then he remembered.

Van's fingers hovered over the keyboard. The blinking cursor dared him to make a decision. After a pause, he typed: *Charli?*

Send.

The bathroom mirror showed him a face that didn't look rested. His hair was doing an impersonation of a minor explosion, and his eyes were still rimmed with sleep. From the kitchen, he heard voices. Pete was up, singing his off-key holiday anthem about Santa coming down the chimney. Van caught the scent of pancake batter sizzling in butter.

Pete called them his world-famous pancakes. They were more like the world's okayest pancakes. The man made them with joy, so Van never said anything.

His phone buzzed. This time it wasn't a text. His heart answered before his brain could. He stared at the screen as if it were slowly waking up.

"Hello?"

"Are you awake?" Her voice. Charli's voice. "That was stupid," she blurted before he could speak. "Can we meet up?"

"Uh... now?"

"There's a café on the west side. The Coffee Place. You know it?"

"Yeah." *(Nope. Never heard of it.)*

"Can you be there in an hour?"

Something inside him twisted. It wasn't nerves, not exactly. It was something else. A warning bell.

"Is something wrong?" he asked.

Silence. Then, with a small breath:

"An hour?"

The same fog he'd been wading through since waking up—was it tangled around her too? Maybe she needed answers as badly as he did. Maybe she didn't want to be alone with the memory of that world.

Maybe she just needed him to say yes.

"Yeah," he said.

The line went dead. A moment later, a text arrived. A pin drop for *The Coffee Place.*

VAN WASN'T USUALLY one to care what he wore or change unless he had to. His general philosophy was: if it didn't smell, it would sell. But Charli had seen him last night. The shirt he was still wearing was like a crumpled badge of slept-in defeat.

He stripped off his belt and dumped his pockets onto the bed. Something brushed against his fingers inside the side pocket of his cargo pants. Slowly, he reached in and pulled it free.

Ring-a-ding.

Van dropped onto the bed like he'd just run too far and too hard. He stared at the green hat in his hands. The one he'd grabbed during the panic. The one that had set everything off. The one from inside the glasses.

It was impossible. But there it was. Here. In his room.

The edges of reality buckled. His thoughts spilled over each other like too much liquid in a glass. The fog that had been creeping around him since the party thickened into a swirling haze.

He held the hat tighter, like squeezing it might tether him to something solid. Something real. But nothing about this was real.

Except the hat.

DOWNTOWN WAS DRESSED for the season. Christmas lights sparkled in the trees. Glittering ornaments dangled from lamp posts, swaying in the morning breeze. Storefronts displayed elaborate scenes—gingerbread villages, train sets circling snowy towns, mannequins wrapped in tinsel.

It was the kind of neighborhood where kids pointed at window displays and tourists snapped selfies beneath wreath-covered archways. A place thick with cinnamon smells and carol melodies. A holiday hub.

Van parked in front of a video game store and killed the engine. And there, tucked between a boutique pet store and a bookshop called *Wyrm & Whimsy,* was a little café.

The Coffee Place looked like it had lost a battle with time. The red letters on the window were faded and flaking, parts of the name completely gone. Through the glass, three mechanical elves stood frozen in a cotton snow display. One raised a wooden mallet. Another dragged a tiny saw across a fake log. The third just stood there, watching the others like a bored manager. Their gears clicked and whirred, but their movements were sluggish, like they'd been winding down for years.

Van reached into his pocket, fingertips brushing soft fabric. He pulled out the elf hat.

Ring-a-ding.

The bell jingled gently, as if it recognized its own kind in the window display. He stared at it for a long second. Then shoved it under the front seat. He didn't know why. It just felt... necessary. Like keeping it in his pocket would mean something he wasn't ready for.

When he opened the door to *The Coffee Place,* a small bell above it chimed. The place smelled like pastries and espresso, with a slow accordion tune drifting through the air like a lullaby for people who didn't sleep well.

The café felt old. Not run-down, but timeless. Like it had always existed, waiting for someone like him to wander in. The bell above the door gave one last, tired ring as it closed behind him.

A few people sat at scattered tables, hunched over laptops, sipping from tall paper cups. The hum of conversation was low and easy. An elderly woman wiped down a nearby table, flinging the rag over her shoulder with practiced flair. She offered Van a kind, crinkly-eyed smile.

"Merry Christmas, young man!" someone called from behind the counter.

The woman there looked like someone had pulled her out of a snow globe. She was round, jolly, and wore her white hair in a thick cloud that matched the whipped cream in the drinks she was serving. Her suspenders barely clung to her broad shoulders, holding up a pair of red trousers that might've belonged to Santa on a casual day.

"What can I get you this morning?" she asked with an accent that sounded part German, part fairy tale.

Van shook his head. The smell of banana bread curled around him, but his stomach turned in quiet rebellion. He couldn't imagine eating anything ever again.

A guy in a bright orange bicycle helmet stepped up beside him and ordered a tall cappuccino with soy milk and a drizzle of honey. Van stepped aside, letting him pass, and scanned the room. A wave of heat rushed up his chest. He blinked, just to make sure he wasn't hallucinating.

There she was. Charli was sitting in the corner, next to a window frosted with paper snowflakes, waving at him like they hadn't survived a surreal fever dream together. Her eyes looked tired. She hadn't changed clothes.

Same shirt. Same jeans.

Van's nerves scrambled. If he'd kept the same clothes on too, maybe they could've laughed about it. Bonded over it. *You're wearing the same thing? We should get married!*

Her hair was tucked awkwardly beneath a faded baseball cap, like she was trying not to be seen. It felt like a scene from a spy novel, two teenagers playing roles they didn't quite believe in, caught between the ordinary and something far stranger.

A plate of banana bread sat untouched in front of her. Two paper cups sat on the table. One directly in front of her, the other opposite, waiting.

"I didn't know if you liked cream or sugar, or..." she said, motioning vaguely toward the cup. "So, it's just black."

"What is?"

"The coffee."

"Oh."

He picked it up, took a cautious sip. Lukewarm. Bitter. She'd been sitting there a while. Even if the coffee was hot and fresh, it wouldn't have helped. Gross.

He set the cup down. "Are you okay?"

She didn't answer right away. Her shoulders were hunched forward, her fingers drumming lightly on the edge of the table. There was a nervous rhythm to her that hadn't been there before.

"You texted at 3:30 last night," he said quietly. "I just thought—"

"Someone was in my room."

Her voice was quiet, almost flat. Her eyes flicked up to meet his for a second, then dropped again. Van leaned in, unsure if he'd heard her right.

"What do you mean?"

"I think someone was looking for something."

"Like... Marla?"

She shook her head. Lips pressed tight. Whatever this was, it wasn't about a sleepover.

Van didn't press. He didn't have to. The same chill that had crept into his bones the night before came back now, stronger. He felt it coil in his stomach.

"Was that when you texted?" he asked.

"Yeah."

"Do you know who it was?"

"No."

She wasn't being rude. Just holding herself together.

The café sounds carried on around them. Cups clinked. Laptops clicked. The bell over the door rang again as a couple walked in, laughing about parking meters. It all felt impossibly normal. Too normal. Like the world didn't know what was unraveling just beneath its surface.

Van rubbed his eyes and let out a sharp breath. "I think there was someone in my room, too."

"You're just saying that."

"No."

He didn't look at her while he spoke. He told her about Lenny at the door. The scratching. The closet. How the clothes were damp. Covered in snow. How they'd been pulled from hangers like someone was searching through them in a rush.

"I didn't ask Pete if Lenny went outside last night," he added. "Didn't need to."

He knew that wasn't it. Just like she knew.

"I had snow in my room, too," she whispered. "And something was in my closet."

Van felt it crash over him. He didn't need the details. He could picture it. Charli waking up in the dark, her dog missing, the sound of something shifting inside the closet. Something not supposed to be there.

"You said those glasses were experimental," Van muttered. "We shouldn't have put them on. We don't even know what they were supposed to do. They said *Christmas presence* on them, and... and... I mean, you thought it was a game, and I thought it was a game. But maybe..."

He trailed off, rubbing his eyes. The words caught in his throat. The truth was heavy, and saying it might make it real.

"Maybe we should tell your dad. He might know something. Maybe when we put those glasses on, it triggered something. Like some kind of system. A defense. And now someone's looking for whatever's in them."

Charli didn't move. Her face lost all its color, going pale like the paper cup in her hands. Van recognized that expression. It was the same hollow look he'd worn when he broke his mom's favorite ornament and had to confess. That awful twist in your stomach when you know what's coming but still have to walk into it.

"He's going to be so mad. I don't want anything to happen to either of us. I don't want us to get into trouble. It was just supposed to be a game. I heard him talking about it, and that's why I went looking for them. It was supposed to be the best game ever."

"Best game ever." Van let out a brittle laugh. "Right."

It had been something. Not a game. Not really. Not anymore.

They fell silent again, the moment stretching between them like thin glass. The banana bread sat untouched. The coffee in their hands cooled.

Van stiffened. He didn't know why at first. A prickling sensation touched the back of his neck.

A man stood across the room. Short. Round. Wrapped in a thick, weather-beaten coat. His beard was enormous, puffed out like a storm cloud, covering most of his face. Only his eyes and the tip of his red, knobby nose were visible.

He wasn't doing anything. Just standing there.

Van felt a chill crawl across his spine. The man didn't fit. Not with the rest of the café. Not with the quiet. Not with anything.

He didn't move. He simply stared, as if he'd been waiting there a long time.

But Van had a lot on his mind. Too many emotions doing cannonballs.

"I'm having trouble remembering everything that happened," he admitted, rubbing his forehead.

"Me, too."

"But I do remember when we were in that toy room, or workshop, or whatever it was. I grabbed that green hat. You remember? That's when the alarm went off. Like something got triggered. Like I wasn't supposed to take it. And I think... I think they were chasing us to get it back."

He paused to let it sink in, his voice dropping.

"And maybe this sounds crazy, but... I've been thinking... maybe whoever was in our rooms last night was looking for the hat."

The words tumbled out faster than he could process them. He didn't look at Charli at first, afraid of what her face might say. But when he finally glanced over, she wasn't wide-eyed or horrified. She looked like she was processing. Like she was turning the idea over in her mind, testing it from every angle. She wasn't convinced. Not yet. But she hadn't dismissed him, either.

"I've got to tell you something," Van said. "And it's going to be hard to believe."

"Nothing can surprise me at this point."

"Like really hard."

"Okay."

"Well..." He looked down at his hands, gathering courage. "I slept in the clothes I wore last night. And when I was changing this morning, I reached into my pocket and, well..." He shrugged. "I found a hat."

"Yeah. Okay."

"The elf hat."

"All right."

She leaned forward slightly, still not getting it. Van widened his eyes. Gave her a slow nod. Charli leaned back, her expression shifting.

"You mean—"

"It was in my pocket." He let the words hang, let the silence do the rest. "When we were being chased, I put the hat in my pocket so the bell wouldn't ring. And that's when we escaped. But it was still there this morning, Charli. In my pocket."

She shook her head and laughed. "What do you mean?"

"I mean... the elf hat was in my pocket. A real one. The same one I took."

"That's not possible."

"I know."

Charli gave a quick, nervous smile. "You're not joking."

"I'm not joking."

"Where is it?"

Van hesitated. "It's in the car."

"Why wouldn't you bring it in here?"

He shook his head. "I don't know. I panicked. I chucked it under the front seat."

"And you're sure it's the same hat?"

"I don't have a bunch of elf hats lying around the house, Charli. Unless you or Jace or Marla are playing some kind of prank, then yeah, it was the hat. It had the little bell on it. I don't know where else it would've come from. I've never seen anything like it before. Not outside that place."

"It's okay. I'm sorry."

Van swallowed, the tension still lodged in his throat. Everything felt upside down. None of it made sense.

But Charli's voice was soft. Her eyes didn't flinch.

If this was all some elaborate joke, then the Oscar goes to her. Her hands were shaking. He could see it, plain as day, but couldn't bring himself to say anything.

He wanted to reach across the table. Just take her hand. Let her know she wasn't alone.

But he didn't. He couldn't.

That wasn't him. He wasn't the kind of person who knew what to say or how to act in moments like this. He knew where he stood on the social ladder. And Charli? She wasn't just a few rungs above. She was on an entirely different ladder.

What right did he have to hold her hand?

He waited for her to speak, hoping the words would break the spell.

Then the short, fat man who'd been watching them from across the café walked past their table. Van almost didn't register him at first. He was lost in his own thoughts, but something caught his eye. The man's feet. They were... off.

Too long. Too wide. And the shoes didn't look like shoes at all.

Van stared. The man didn't seem to care. He reached for a curtain at the back of the café and slipped behind it without a glance. A small sign above it read, *Employees Only*.

A cold prickle crawled up the back of Van's neck. "Did you see that?"

"Will you go with me to tell my dad? I just want to get it over with. Or maybe we should wait until after Christmas. You know, so we don't ruin the holidays. Maybe after New Year's..."

She kept talking, not really looking at him. Her words tumbled out in a rush. What if something was wrong with them? What if the glasses did something to their minds? What if they were unraveling?

Van had been right. This wasn't a game. It never was. And if they waited too long, what if there wasn't a way back?

Van was still watching the curtain. His brain was stuck on those feet. And the ears. They had stuck out strangely, angled like something that didn't quite belong.

"Charli," he whispered. "Did you see that guy who just walked by?"

"What?"

"I know this is going to sound weird, but he had..." Van stretched his hands far apart, like he was describing a record fish he'd caught. "His feet were like... and his ears were all..."

"What?"

"He's been watching us. From across the room. And then he just walked by, like it was nothing." He swallowed, his mouth suddenly dry. "Look, I'm going to check the room where he went. After that, we can go tell your dad. I just... I just want to check something real quick."

Before he could finish, Charli did something completely unexpected. She stood up without a word.

Van stared at her. He wasn't sure if she'd heard a single thing he'd said, but she walked straight toward the *Employees Only* doorway, her steps steady. Like she'd already made up her mind.

Van hesitated. Then, almost without deciding to, he stood.

Something about this moment felt like it mattered. Like it would change things.

THE CURTAIN PARTED with a soft rustle. Beyond it was a room dimly lit. The glow from the café behind them filtered in but died just inside the entrance.

It was a pantry. Boxes of loose-leaf tea. Burlap sacks of coffee beans. Stacked bags of flour and sugar. The air was thick with the cozy scent of cinnamon and vanilla, but layered beneath was a scent like dust and copper. Like an attic sealed shut for years.

Van followed Charli in. The curtain dropped behind him with a whisper, sealing them in.

The sudden quiet was suffocating. No clinking dishes. No music. No voices.

Only the scent of pastries.

Van's fingers fumbled for his phone. He unlocked the screen, and the flashlight cut a white beam through the dark. The shadows leapt back.

No one was there. No movement. Just crates and shelves and tin canisters stacked high.

Goosebumps rose along his arms. Something was wrong. Not visibly wrong. Not in any way he could explain. But he felt it, pressing in around the edges.

His light swept across the room. The shadows it cast were jagged and unnatural, like claws stretching across the floor and up the walls.

Charli stood beside him, arms wrapped around herself, eyes darting like she was waiting for something to pounce.

Van swept the beam again. There had to be something. A clue. A door.

He'd seen the strange little man come in here. The one with the feet and the ears. The one who hadn't looked back.

It felt like a puzzle. A hidden-object game. Move the right bag of flour, press a button hidden in the shelves, and a secret door would creak open to somewhere else. A new level. A hidden room.

He shook his head and thought, *This isn't a game.*

His foot nudged something on the floor. It slid a few inches with a soft scrape.

Charli didn't notice. She was too busy gripping his arm, pulling him toward the curtain.

"Look," Van said.

It was a tiny box. Wrapped in green paper. A red ribbon tied into a flawless bow like a Christmas present. Maybe a little bigger than a tennis ball. Out of place in a pantry with dusty shelves and sacks of flour.

"Let's go," Charli whispered. Her fingers tightened around his sleeve.

"Wait."

"No." She shook her head, sharp and fast. "There's nobody in here, Van. And we are not opening that. We're already in enough trouble. We need to leave."

But Van pulled free. He didn't know why. It surprised even him. Curiosity had sunk its claws in.

He ignored the chill climbing his spine. Reached for the tiny tag tucked under the bow. His phone's beam glinted off it as he lifted it gently.

Neat, looping handwriting. *For Charli and Van.*

He looked up with wide eyes and half a smile. Before he could say anything, a crash rang out from the café. Like something heavy had fallen and shattered.

Charli spun toward the curtain, hands trembling. Her breathing turned shallow, quick.

Van was kneeling beside the box, the weight of the moment on him. His instincts screamed to run, to leave this creepy, twisted room where a strange, little man left a present for them. Because it had to be him, the fat little man. Who wasn't in the room anymore.

They should turn around and leave, tell Charli's dad everything.

But then... what was in the box?

"Van—"

"I know what you're going to say." He was calm, even as his heart pounded. "But someone wanted us to find this. It has our names on it, Charli."

"We should leave," she said again.

Van nodded. He heard her. He believed her.

But as she turned back to the curtain, distracted by the noise outside, the box sat there like it was waiting for him.

His fingers brushed the lid.

A breath. A pause. Then he lifted it—

Light exploded out of it. Blinding white.

They gasped, raising their arms to shield their faces as the pantry lurched. The air snapped cold like winter blew into the room. Their breath fogged in front of them.

Snowflakes burst from the box, silvery and perfect, vanishing before they hit the ground. The room twisted. Shifted. A gust of wind stirred the curtain, tugging it restlessly.

Van scrambled to shut the lid, but it wouldn't budge. It was like the box itself was resisting, unwilling to be closed.

The light kept pouring out, washing over the room like a tidal wave.

Then came the voices. Faint, but unmistakably clear. They echoed from inside the box.

"Van—" Charli started.

But she didn't finish.

The pull came all at once. The magnetic force shooting out of the gift suddenly reversed. Van snapped forward. He gasped as his feet left the ground, stomach lurching, balance gone. The air bent and twisted around him, the walls of the pantry stretching like rubber.

He reached out, whether to push the box away or grab Charli, he didn't know.

But it was too late. The cold hit next. Not just on his skin, but in his bones. In his blood.

It crawled up his spine and into his lungs. His breath came out in jagged clouds. His fingers went numb.

Everything around him expanded.

The shelves. The bags. The light. They all stretched outward, becoming distant, becoming unreal.

Time lost meaning. The sounds of the café faded completely. No more dishes. No more footsteps. No more world.

Only silence. Only cold.

And then Charli and Van were gone.

As if they had never been there at all.

3

When Van was fourteen, his appendix burst.

He could still remember the anesthesia mask being pressed to his face, the deep breath he took. And then nothing. No fade to black. No drift into sleep. Just a sudden cut, like someone had sliced a scene from his life and thrown it on the floor. One moment he was there, in the operating room, and the next he was waking up somewhere else.

It was that same feeling now. One second, in the pantry. The next, somewhere else. No transition. No warning. No sense of time passing.

This room was bigger. Much bigger. And colder. The air was like being wrapped in a fog made of ice. The ceiling hung low, and the walls shimmered with a bluish sheen, slick and smooth like frozen glass. A battered couch leaned against one side of the room, a desk and wooden chair tucked into a corner. A coat rack stood nearby, weighted with scarves, coats, and knitted stocking caps.

There were no windows. No doors.

Van's brain scrambled to make sense of the shift. It didn't. It couldn't. The human mind wasn't made for teleportation. For being ripped out of one place and dropped in another. He turned, eyes darting, heart hammering in his chest.

Charli stood nearby, her mouth slightly open, her eyes wide. Her pupils were so dilated her irises had almost disappeared. She looked at Van like she was seeing him for the first time.

And then, like flakes of snow settling on glass, the realization came.

She gasped.

Her body wobbled like her knees had turned to liquid. She clutched at her chest, her breath catching. Her other hand shot out blindly and latched onto Van's arm, nails digging in.

"Breathe," he said. "Count to six and breathe." He demonstrated, drawing a slow inhale through his nose. Holding it. "Just like that."

Pete had taught him that. Breathing techniques from some meditative workshop he'd taken in college. Breath equals calm. Calm equals control. Van didn't know if it actually worked. But it was something.

Charli mirrored him, breath hitching, then steadied. She was trembling but listening. She took another breath.

Then she turned toward the empty air in front of them and shouted.

"Hello? Is anybody there? Help!"

Her voice echoed, bouncing off the icy walls.

They stood on a round rug, wool or felt, something thick. The only barrier between them and the frozen floor. Van stepped forward, meaning to knock on the wall or test for a door.

The moment his foot left the rug and touched the ice, it slipped.

He fell sideways with a startled grunt and caught himself on the coat rack. The whole thing wobbled, but didn't fall.

Charli was hugging herself now, shivering. Without thinking, Van yanked a scarf from the rack and gave it to her. Then a hat. Then the heaviest coat he could find. He draped it over her shoulders.

She clutched the coat tighter around herself, lips trembling, teeth chattering.

He hesitated. Wondered if he should put his arm around her. Just for warmth. For survival.

Before he could decide, he saw something move. Not in front of him. Off to the side.

A ripple in the wall. Someone stepped through it and into the room.

The man from the café. The short one. The round one. Like a friendly cartoon character made real.

As he passed through the wall it became obvious. This wasn't a man. And not totally human.

For one, his ears stuck out at odd angles. Sharp, pointed things that peeked through a messy mop of brown hair. And he wasn't walking, not exactly. His feet, enormous and bare, glided over the icy floor. Each was the size of a snowshoe, with tufts of wiry hair curling over his toes like frostbitten moss.

Most people would've called him an elf. What else could he be?

He came to a stop beside the tiny gift box. The same gift that had hoovered them into this room, the one addressed to Charli and Van. It now sat neatly on the frozen floor.

With visible effort, he bent over his round belly, scooped it up, and tucked it into the inner lining of his coat.

"Well, you found the coats," he said in a bright, almost musical voice. The kind of voice that didn't match his body at all. "You should put one on, too."

The way he said it made Van's stomach twist. It wasn't a suggestion. It wasn't even friendly advice. It was a statement. Like he knew Van would be needing one. Like he wasn't going anywhere soon.

"Let's start by breathing," the elf said, raising his shoulders with exaggerated calm. He inhaled deeply through his nose, a loud whoosh, then sighed out a slow, theatrical exhale. "Nice and easy. Try it."

Van scanned the room. It already felt different.

That lamp. Had it always been there? The framed pictures on the wall?

There hadn't been a window. But now one stretched wide across the far wall, frosted around the edges, revealing a vast tundra bathed in pale, directionless light. No sun. No moon. Just a still, glowing expanse that looked endless. Empty.

"I'm Nog, by the way," the elf said cheerfully. "You don't have to sit. But maybe you'd like something to drink? A little eggnog? A cookie?"

Van glanced toward a table that hadn't been there a moment ago. It now stood neatly against the wall, holding a plate of cookies and a full glass pitcher of golden eggnog.

Neither he nor Charli moved toward it.

"Suit yourselves." He glided over to the table, plucked a *cookie*, and bit into it with a delighted hum. Crumbs tumbled down the front of his tunic. "You're missing out."

Van barely heard him. Charli still clung to the coat, knuckles white around the sleeves. Her face had gone pale, eyes unfocused. Van guided her to the couch. She sank down, slow and heavy, her expression distant and quiet.

Nog dusted his hands off and clapped once. "Right. Introductions. Sullivan Holloway. You go by Van. Charlotte Marie McNichols. You prefer Charli. I like that name, by the way. Suits you."

Charli gave no sign she heard him.

"You two know each other," he went on, "but not that well. Just properly met last night. Before that? Not a single real conversation. You're both mostly nice, but a little naughty. Then again, who isn't? Nobody's just one or the other. That'd be weird. Unnatural. Honestly, a little creepy."

He leaned forward, rubbing his hands together.

"Now," Nog said, "do you know why you're here?"

"Where *is* here?" Van said.

"Ah, yes. That." Nog tapped his fingers together, slowly, watching them with a grin that was more knowing than kind. "You're waiting to wake up, aren't you? Thinking this is some elaborate dream. A trick of the mind. Classic. I've seen it before. Problem is, you won't wake up. Because you're not asleep."

Van's jaw tightened. "I don't think so."

"I get it. One minute you're in a cozy little café, trying to deal with real life and the next, *poof*. Ice floors, magic portals. An elf stuffing his face with *cookies*. It's a lot to take in."

"So... this is real?" Charli said.

"As real as it gets, young lady." He clapped once, the sound oddly loud in the slick, echoing room. "All right. Let's cut to it. *He* brought you here for a reason."

His voice shifted, a reverent note threading through it. Charli and Van looked at each other. Van knew who Nog was talking about. It was Charli's dad. Mr. McNichols. Who else would know this much about the glasses.

But Charli wasn't getting it. "Who brought us here?" she said.

"Who do you think?"

The twinkle in Nog's eyes flickered. Faded slightly. He sighed, then nodded to himself, as if understanding the depth of their disbelief.

"Totally normal," he said. "Kids get older, they start doubting. Then one day, they just... stop believing. Happens all the time. Usually around ten."

He pointed at Van.

"You? Eight years old. Caught your mom wrapping a gift that looked suspiciously familiar. The next morning, you stopped believing."

Then he turned to Charli.

"And you, ten. A kid at school told you he wasn't real. You laughed along, even though it hurt. Because you didn't want to be made fun of."

Nog shook his head, his expression oddly sincere.

"It's an epidemic. Everyone's got a phone. Everyone's got proof. Everyone knows everything, but believes in nothing. Used to be simple. A letter. A chimney. A *cookie* on a plate. But now?" He let out a long, low whistle. "Now it's a miracle if a kid makes it to five before figuring it out. If it were up to me..."

"Santa Claus?" Van cut in. "Are you talking about Santa Claus?"

"Of course. Who did you...?" Nog looked back and forth. "See, this is what I'm talking about."

Van stared, stunned. The words sounded ridiculous in his head, but in this cold, impossible place they seemed almost normal.

Charli didn't react at all. Her lips were slightly parted, her breath thin and uneven. Her eyes, wide and raw, stayed fixed on Nog like she was trying to blink him out of existence.

But she couldn't. Because this was still happening.

"Well," Nog said, bouncing slightly on his toes, "as you surely know, it's Christmas Eve. And whether you believe in Santa or not, he's coming to town. Right now, as we speak, the list is being checked. Presents are ready for trees. Stockings to be filled."

He pointed at them both.

"And you two? Despite some questionable choices, you made the nice list. But barely."

He wagged a stubby finger, half-scolding, half-playful.

"But make no mistake... you were naughty. Very naughty." Nog's eyes twinkled as he waited for their reaction. Van and Charli remained still. "You do know why you're here, right?" he asked.

"I do," Charli said.

"Oh yes, good. For a second there—"

"Because we took my dad's glasses," Charli said quickly, the words tumbling out. "I swear, we were going to tell him. We were. We said we'd come clean and that's exactly what we were going to do."

Nog nodded slowly. "Yes. I heard that part. That's why you're still on the nice list. But," he held up a warning finger, "you shouldn't have taken the glasses. They weren't yours. Still, you were going to be honest. Santa knows that. He always knows."

He paused, watching them both.

"But I have to ask... what did you think the glasses were doing?"

"It's a VR game," Charli said. "Next generation. My dad works at *Avocado*."

"A game?" He scratched at his beard, thick fingers digging through the snowy curls. "One more question. Santa would like to know the answer. We all would. It's the reason you're here." He leaned forward. "Where is the hat?"

Van and Charli weren't expecting the turn in conversation. "What hat?" Van said.

Nog's face fell in mock disappointment. "Now that's naughty. Let's not pretend. You both used the glasses to access the workshop. Not just any workshop, mind you. The *Toymaker's* workshop. And unfortunately, her hat was unattended when you arrived."

He let out a weary sigh, clearly wounded by the breach of trust.

"She never does that. Not in all her years. But then again, she doesn't expect uninvited guests to waltz in and help themselves, either."

Nog seemed to know a lot about them. He spoke with certainty, with detail. But somehow, strangely, he didn't know where the hat was. That would explain the present situation.

Van felt something in his chest. Not just guilt or fear. It was pressure. The urge to tell the truth warred with something deeper. An instinct to be careful with what he said next. He had no idea where they were or how to get home (if, that is, they weren't dreaming, which was still an option).

"I don't have it," Van said.

"Of course, you don't. If you did, you wouldn't be here and we wouldn't be having this conversation." He glided forward, closer. "So. Where is it?"

Van glanced at Charli. "It's at my house," he said finally. "Under my pillow."

"I see." He stroked his beard again. "And the dog?"

"Lenny? He won't hurt you."

"That's not what I'm asking."

"What are you asking, then?"

"I'm asking," Nog said, oddly serious, "is your dog… *cool*?"

"It sounds like you're asking if he'll hurt you."

Nog didn't smile. "Answer the question, please."

"Yeah. He's *cool*."

Nog seemed to consider that with utmost gravity. He tapped his cheek, muttering something under his breath. His lips moved, but the words weren't in English. They weren't in any language Van recognized. They sounded warped, layered, like two voices speaking at once. One high, one impossibly low.

"Very well. We'll retrieve the hat from under your pillow. We appreciate your cooperation. You don't realize how important this is."

Van wasn't entirely sure why he lied. Things were so strange and going too fast. He was stalling for time, that's why he did it. He wasn't a liar, by nature. It happened, but not as often as others. That's why guilt began gnawing at his insides.

"What if you don't find it?" he asked. He paused, then added, "I mean... what if it's gone?"

"Gone? Why would it be gone?"

"I don't know. What if someone took it?"

"Well, that would be a problem."

Nog's cheerful demeanor dimmed. He moved toward the center of the room again, the ice beneath his feet humming with the faintest musical resonance.

"You see, that hat... it's not just fabric and thread. It's one of the main sources of *Christmas spirit*. A conduit. A vessel. It catches the joy of the season and radiates it outward. Without it... Christmas couldn't go on. Not properly."

Charli stiffened. "What do you mean, couldn't go on?"

"Christmas isn't just about presents, young lady. Sure, presents are a big part of it. When you're young, they're everything. But as you grow older, you begin to realize... it's so much more than that."

He raised his hand, palm up, fingers spread wide, as though cradling something invisible and impossibly fragile.

"The spirit of Christmas flows through families, through friend-ships, through entire worlds. Universes. I may be exaggerating just a smidge. *Christmas* wouldn't vanish overnight without the Toymaker's hat. But it would *fade*."

The corners of his mouth turned downward.

"People wouldn't care as much. They'd go through the motions, sure. But the spark would be missing. The lights would be a little dimmer. The songs wouldn't hit the same. The laughter would fade a few notes too soon. The air would lose that shimmer. Not all at once. It would creep in slowly. Subtly. But make no mistake, if the Toymak-er's hat isn't returned... that's exactly what will happen."

For the first time, Van felt the significance of what they'd done. This wasn't just about borrowing something from her dad. It wasn't just about sneaking around or bending the rules. This *sounded* way bigger than a company secret.

Someone had been in his room last night. He hadn't imagined the creaking. The whisper of cold behind the closet door. Someone *had* been searching for the hat, he decided. And they hadn't found it. Because it wasn't in the closet.

Would *Christmas* really fade if he didn't give it back? *Christmas* was everywhere. Commercials, store windows, songs in every hallway. It was huge. It was profitable. A global money machine wouldn't shut down because of one missing hat. Right?

And yet, here they were, standing in a windowless ice room. Talking to an elf.

His gut told him not to hold on—not to give up the hat just yet. Maybe it had something to do with Charli sitting so close to him. Because when this was all over, when everything was said and done, they'd be back at school, and she'd never talk to him again. And maybe he didn't want this to end just yet.

Not maybe. Probably.

"You broke into our houses," Van said. "You went through our closets in the middle of the night while we were sleeping."

Nog skidded to a stop just as he was gliding toward the section of the wall where he'd first entered. He turned slowly, feet scraping softly against the ice.

"And why do you think we did that?"

"That's naughty, don't you think? Breaking into our homes?"

"We didn't enter your homes willy-nilly. We had a very good reason. The Toymaker's hat does not belong to either of you. You took it at the worst possible time."

His tone darkened. The playful glint in his eye faded.

"There are only hours left before Christmas, and the Toymaker is without her hat. Do you understand the consequences? Everything is in motion. The sleigh is being loaded. The reindeer are being fed. It's going to be a very long night, yet the Toymaker—the one who ensures that *Christmas* happens at all—is missing the very thing that allows her to do her job."

He exhaled sharply through his nose. The breath misted in the freezing air. Nog narrowed his eyes at Van.

"Now... is there anything else you'd like to tell me?"

Charli glanced at Van but didn't say a word. She knew exactly where the hat was. So why wasn't she speaking up? Maybe she felt the same gut instinct Van did. That something didn't quite add up. Or maybe, just maybe, she wanted to stay with him a little longer, too.

Probably not. But maybe.

"No," Van said.

Nog studied them in silence, his expression unreadable. Then, with a curt nod, he turned toward the icy tunnel.

"Very well. You two stay here. Keep warm. Stay comfortable. We'll be right back. Once we've retrieved the hat and returned it to its rightful place, we'll send you home. It will be as if you were never here at all."

He paused.

"And you won't remember a thing."

"You're going to erase our memories?" Charli asked.

Nog lifted his hand and waved his fingers through the air in a slow, fluid motion. It looked almost like a magician casting a spell. Or someone practicing a ritual they'd done a thousand times before.

"Whether you believe in Santa Claus or not," he said, "it's not good for people to know what's really going on up here."

"You mean... he's here? Right now?"

"We're on the North Pole. Where else would he be on Christmas Eve?"

Van looked around the room, uncertain of which direction to even point, whether this room was an igloo on the ice or carved from inside it.

"Santa Claus is packing the sleigh right now?"

"Well... I don't know if he's packing—"

"If the sleigh's here, then... we could just go get our presents, right?" Van turned to Charli, his eyes wide with something between sarcasm and desperation. "I mean, you'd believe in Santa if you saw him, right?"

Charli met his gaze, slowly nodding. There was something in her expression. Something small, but growing. The faintest spark of belief flickering to life. If this was a dream (still the odds-on favorite), then Santa Claus would be packing a sleigh. And reindeer would be eating carrots. And elves would be making toys.

That wouldn't prove Santa Claus was real, though. It would, without a doubt, prove this to be a holiday hallucination. Because Van wasn't ten years old anymore.

"I see what you're doing," Nog said. "We don't bring humans to the North Pole to let them pick out their gifts. That's not how this works. Do you really think he'd be pleased if you just walked up there and grabbed the computer you want for Christmas from the sleigh?"

His eyes snapped to Charli.

"Or if you snatched up those Alice Einhorn boots with the fuzzy trim you asked for?"

Van felt his throat tighten. Charli's lips parted, but no words came out. That was exactly what they'd asked for. Those were two pretty good guesses. Not impossible. What teenage boy didn't want his own laptop or the current fashion in boots? If it was a dream, that wouldn't be hard to know at all. But still…

Nog smirked. With a wink, he turned and glided effortlessly across the ice, his coat trailing behind him like a cape. Casting a final glance over his shoulder, he said, "Merry, merry. I'll be back."

THE WALL where Nog had disappeared was solid. Van knocked on it anyway, half-expecting it to shimmer or blink out like a hologram. But it didn't. It was as real and unyielding as granite. He let his forehead rest against it for a second, breathing out in a foggy sigh.

If he'd told the truth, they wouldn't be waiting to wake up or go home, whatever was happening here. Either way, they'd be back in their beds. No more mystery, no more questions, just like Nog promised.

Charli was curled up on the couch, her arms wrapped tightly around her knees. She rocked gently, the motion subtle but constant. Van wasn't exactly calm. His pulse thudded in his ears. His hands wouldn't stop twitching. He wanted to sit next to her, to lean into each other so their shoulders touched. Maybe they'd get tired enough for their heads to touch.

It wasn't much longer before he decided he was going to say it. Out loud. Shout it if he had to. Tell whoever was listening where the hat was. That it was under the front seat of his car. Parked outside The Coffee Shop.

If someone needed to be punished, let it be him. Just let Charli wake up or go home. He didn't care which.

Before he could get the words out, the air around them began to change.

It started as a faint hum, barely noticeable, like the low whine of electronics warming up. Then it shifted. A crackling static swept through the room like invisible lightning, prickling against his skin. His hair stood on end.

The sound deepened into something stranger, a wet sizzling hiss, like meat on a skillet or wires melting from heat.

A single point of golden light flared into existence midair. From it unraveled a golden thread, twirling and swaying as if caught in a breeze no one could feel. The thread flicked once, then split wide open, like curtains pulled open on a stage.

Beyond was pure darkness. And from the darkness... an elf stepped through.

If it had been anyone other than an elf, Van might've been surprised. This one looked just like Nog with the same mischievous glint in her eyes. Only she didn't have a beard. Her hair was woven into a thick braid that hung like a heavy rope.

She moved with purpose, brisk and impatient, her expression caught somewhere between casual indifference and low-level annoyance.

Van didn't need to guess why she was here. She'd been sent to deal with his lie. Of that, he was certain.

"Everything checked out," she announced. Her voice carried an officious edge, like someone used to giving orders at a help desk. "We'd like to apologize for the inconvenience. It's Christmas, after all, and we hate doing this. We want you to have a very merry Christmas, so if you're ready, we can take you home now."

Charli straightened, then stood. "You... found the hat?"

The elf's expression remained neutral. "I didn't say that. I said everything checked out. Now, let's get you home."

"Where's Nog?" Van said.

"Drowning in paperwork," she said, flicking her hand. "This is a big operation, you know. North Pole. Millions of presents. Global delivery system. And with Christmas right around the corner? Let's just say there are a lot of elves with a lot of things to do."

She sighed heavily, like explaining any further would physically exhaust her.

"Anyway, I've got a job, and standing around here isn't it. If you don't want to stick around any longer, follow me."

Van's instincts prickled. She sounded helpful. Reasonable. But something about her manner felt off. If they were going to be sent home, wasn't it supposed to happen after the hat was found? Wasn't that the whole point?

"I want to go home," Charli said.

Van looked at her. Her back was straight. Her jaw set. There was resolve in her voice, something that hadn't been there before. It weakened his hesitation.

"Yeah. Me too."

The elf waved toward the black curtain of space that had appeared earlier. It yawned like a tear in reality, swallowing light around its edges like a shadow with teeth. It felt eerily familiar. The same kind of portal that had sucked them from the café pantry into this surreal, snow-drenched world.

"Why aren't we using the present?" Van said.

The elf paused, just for a second. Barely noticeable. But he caught it.

"Oh. Well... it ran out of juice or something. I don't know, I'm not an engineer," she said with a dismissive shrug. "I just know we can't use it. Anyway, this is better. Faster."

Faster? How could it be faster?

Van opened his mouth to question her, but before he could say a word, the elf nudged them forward.

Charli stepped into the dark curtain first. The void swallowed her instantly. Her hand shot back toward Van, instinctive and desperate. He grabbed it without thinking. Her fingers were cold as ice. She pulled him in. Or maybe the portal pulled them both.

His stomach flipped. The world vanished. There was no floor, no sky, no sensation at all. Only a sucking pressure, like a universal vacuum cleaner. Maybe this was how he woke up from dreams and just never remembered. It felt something like that.

The last sound he heard before the darkness closed over his ears was a voice, distant and urgent, echoing like it came from underwater. A weird way for a dream to end.

It sounded like Nog shouting for them to come back.

4

When they stumbled through the black curtain, one thing was immediately clear.

They weren't home. Not even close.

The elf glided in behind them, unbothered by the jarring transition, moving with the ease of someone who had done this a thousand times. Without breaking stride, she reached up and plucked a small brass button from the air, as if it had been waiting there just for her.

With a practiced flick of her wrist, she opened a flap on her coat. Then another. Then another. Each flap revealed a smaller, more hidden pocket nested inside the last. She slid the brass button into one of them and pressed it firmly closed with her fingers. Then, in a flurry of motion, she fastened each flap again, neat and secure.

"This is just a pit stop," she said, raising a hand to cut off any protest. "Protocol for going home. We've got to check in, file the paperwork. Administration is the worst."

The air around them was thick, motionless. It wasn't pitch black, but the darkness here was different. Dense and unwilling to lift, like a heavy velvet drape drawn tight over the world. It soaked into their clothes, their hair, their lungs.

Slowly, the scenery began to emerge from the gloom. Behind

them loomed a rock wall. Tall, jagged, and cracked like it had been scarred by centuries. The stone was cold and sharp, and its presence looming.

Ahead of them stretched a massive tar pit. Its surface was black and glassy, but not reflective. It absorbed all light. Not even the tiny lightning bugs hovering above it could throw a shimmer across the ooze. Their delicate green lights simply blinked into the void and disappeared.

The trees surrounding the pit looked dead, or close to it. Their branches were crooked and brittle, clawing at the sky. Their grayish leaves drooped like they'd given up long ago. The air was filled with the hum of insects, but it wasn't natural. Just one long, low, relentless note, like a warning tone stretched out forever.

"The king will be down in a sec. He wanted you to come up to the room, but" — she gave a quick pat to the flap where the button had disappeared — "that's not how this thing works. By the way, him coming down to greet you? That never happens. Like ever."

She kept talking, her words floating off into the gloom. Van was locked on the tar pit. It looked alive. Not in a biological sense, but in the way it refused to be ignored. It demanded attention through its silence, its stillness. Even the bugs gave it a wide berth, bobbing and swerving high above it like nervous satellites.

"Where are we?" Charli asked.

The elf held up a dented metal bucket. "Chocolate?"

"What—no. We just want to go home."

"These things take time, sweetheart," the elf replied. "You remember the paperwork, right? You can't just haul a couple of warmbloods across the universe without some bureaucracy. You know, duplicates. Triplicates. It's a whole process." She clicked her tongue. "You should be grateful you made it this far. Some people don't make it back."

"What do you want from us?" Van blurted, the pressure that he might not be dreaming building.

"Didn't you hear me? Duplicates, triplicates... do you even know what a triplicate is? I feel like I'm talking to a couple of rocks. No offense. Patience is a—"

"You want the hat," Van cut in.

The elf scoffed. A short, sharp laugh that felt more like a blade than a joke. "Oh, now that you mention it—"

"I already told you where it is."

"Yeah," she said. "But that was a lie. Wanna try again?"

There was something deeply unsettling about her. Unlike Nog, she wasn't hiding behind politeness. She didn't care about manners or appearances. She had been too quick to usher them through the portal with vague promises of going home. And now here they were, stranded in a place that reeked of secrets and rot.

"You're not with Nog, are you?" Charli said.

The elf sputtered for a second, caught off guard. Her mouth opened and closed, fishlike, before she scoffed again.

"You're accusing me of helping you escape? Guilty as charged, m'lady. Trust me, he wasn't going to send you home. I think you know why."

She pretended to wipe invisible dust from her generous belly, checked her nails. As if she couldn't care less.

"So we're stuck here until you get the hat," Charli said.

"Something like that. One of those back-scratching deals. You know what I mean?"

"How do you know we were lying about the hat? You weren't even in the room when Van told Nog where it is."

The elf twitched. Then, like flipping a switch, she smiled. "I'd normally say it's a secret, but since you're guests..."

She flicked her fingers nonchalantly, as if brushing away lint. Something happened when she did. Tiny motes of light shimmered in the gloom, drifting like glitter stirred in a snow globe. They hung in the thick, humid air, glowing faintly.

Charli stared at them. "You were spying."

"Listening is not a crime. Is it naughty? Yeah. It's what we do." She stepped closer, her bare feet crunching faintly against the brittle, ash-covered ground. "The king's going to want to know about the hat. You might want to start thinking more about that than why the sun is round or how reindeer fly."

The silence that followed was oppressive. The air was a physical weight. Van's breath came slower now. The truth settled in his gut like a stone.

He shouldn't have lied.

None of this made sense. None of it. But that didn't matter. They were here now. Caught in a place that didn't seem to exist on any map, standing on the edge of a tar-black pit with a cold-eyed elf who might have lured them into something far worse than Nog's pleasant disappointment.

Then, from somewhere beyond the trees, deep within the heavy dark, a sharp metallic clang rang through the air.

It echoed like a warning bell.

Van and Charli turned, their eyes drawn upward for the first time.

The towering rock wall loomed above them, an impenetrable mass of jagged, serrated stone. Its ridges caught what little light there was, casting long, blade-like shadows slicing through the fog. At its base, a narrow seam had opened, revealing a dark cavity within the wall. From that hidden passage, a massive, boxy throne creaked into view.

It groaned with movement, its rusted undercarriage whining and clicking like broken clockwork. Metal joints snapped and shuddered as the throne slowly rolled forward, its wheels struggling against the rough, uneven terrain. It moved only ten feet before stuttering to a halt.

The enormous figure seated within it rocked back and forth, clearly irritated. With a disgruntled huff, he stopped trying altogether. The man in the throne was massive.

Vast.

His body spilled across the throne's broad surface like melting wax, folds of flesh pouring over the armrests and pooling at the sides.

It looked less like he was sitting in the chair and more like he had absorbed it. The throne itself groaned beneath the weight.

Atop his head sat a tiny, crooked crown, too small for his swollen skull. It gleamed gold, an oddly pristine contrast to the murky, moonless light that sickened the landscape around them. The crown looked like a toy. A trinket. An afterthought.

Trailing behind the throne came three figures, each of them wrong in some quiet, unspoken way. They moved in absolute synchronization, their steps stiff and mechanical. Their bodies were unnaturally flat, as if they'd been carved from poster board and animated by some clumsy, unseen hand. Their edges were too sharp, too bright, like paper dolls cut from another universe.

The throne came to a final, screeching halt. The metal screamed beneath it. The noise echoed through the pit, bouncing off stone and tar, lingering like a sour note.

The king's eyes, slow and ponderous, moved from Van to Charli. He looked at them as if he were weighing them on an invisible scale. He exhaled. The sound was more furnace than breath.

His meaty fingers twitched. He adjusted his crooked crown with a grunt, then let out a low, guttural gurgle, something bubbling up from beneath one of his many chins like a clogged drain trying to breathe.

"They talk?" he said at last.

"Nerp," muttered the elf.

"What did I tell you, Jelly?" the king grumbled like the rumble of a dying bear. "A lot of naughty in them. Especially that one."

He jabbed a fat finger in Van's direction, the tip wobbling with the motion. His glare was sharp, the accusation plain. Then he looked at Charli.

"Her?" he snorted. "Not so much."

He reached into a shallow bowl embedded in the armrest of his throne. His hand vanished into the pile, then emerged with a fistful of chocolate wafers, which he stuffed into his mouth.

The sound of chewing was wet and thunderous. Like hooves

churning thick mud, each squelch more grotesque than the last. The slurping was obscene, each bite a slap across the silence.

The king seemed to swell larger as he sat, as if the throne were drawing from some hidden reservoir of mass. The three flat figures flanked him in eerie stillness, twitching at intervals like puppets waiting for their next cue.

"Too much goody in her, Jelly," the king mumbled, crumbs clinging to the stubble on his chin. "Call my brother. He can deal with her."

"She's not going anywhere," Van said.

The king stopped chewing mid-bite. The silence that followed was sharp and immediate. Like the air itself had tensed. Crumbs clung to his lips. His jaw remained open, caught between shock and amusement. Then, slowly, deliberately, he turned his head and glared at Jelly.

One eyebrow arched.

"Jelly? You want to—"

"No one talks to the king like that," Jelly said, her voice flat. Almost bored.

The three cardboard-thin figures began to move, their steps disjointed and twitchy, circling around Van and Charli with jerky, marionette precision. Their muttering grew louder. Strange, guttural sounds that grated against the ears like sandpaper dragged across glass. Though unintelligible, the tone was unmistakable.

Their fingers, crackling like firelit parchment, reached for Charli's coat. Tiny snaps accompanied each tug. She swatted at them, trying to keep her balance.

"Did you give them chocolate?" the king asked.

"They didn't want any," Jelly replied.

"Nonsense," the king muttered. "Eat chocolate, kiddos!"

With a lazy flick of his massive hand, he scattered another handful of chocolate wafers into the air. They fluttered around Van and Charli like sad, stale confetti.

"We're not supposed to be here," Van said.

"You're exactly where you're supposed to be." He leaned forward.

His throne groaned beneath him. Folds of flesh shifted like glaciers in motion. "You lied like a pro, son. No hesitation. Not a flicker of doubt. You knew how to play the game, and me likey. You belong here. With us."

"And where exactly are we?" Charli asked.

The king jerked back in his throne, sending a ripple through his entire body. It moved like a wave passing through dough.

"Do we have backbone?" he rumbled. "You were wilting when Noggy was grilling you on the couch. All quiet and sadface. But you didn't rat out your boyfriend when he lied to his face." He nodded with theatrical approval. "There's hope for you, little lady."

"I'm not her boyfriend," Van muttered.

He'd jumped in too fast. Cut Charli off before she had the chance to respond. It would sting a little less if he said. That's what he told himself.

The king exhaled, a puff of air that might've been a laugh, or just a shift in weight.

"To answer your question," he said, "here is here."

"That doesn't answer the question," Charli said.

"Oh, it totally does," the king replied, shoving another cluster of chocolate into his mouth. "Just because you don't like it doesn't make it not an answer, missy."

"'Here is here' is not an answer," Charli snapped. She turned to Jelly. "You promised we'd go home. And now we're here. That was a lie. And you know it."

"Well, lying's sort of what we do," Jelly said.

"You kids want answers? Fine." The king waved his fingers dramatically. "Here's one: there's a nice side and a naughty side. Take a wild guess which one you're on."

He leaned forward again, massive arms resting on his knees, thick fingers gripping the edge.

"Now," he said, slow and heavy, "where's the hat?"

"Will you send us home if we tell you?" Van asked.

"Definitely," the king said without hesitation, raising one chocolate-smeared hand. "Scout's honor."

"I don't believe you."

"Figures. So here's what we're going to do. You're going for a swim in Fudgy Lake. After that, we'll cover you in sprinkles until you look like a doughnut. Then I'll ask again. And if you don't have an answer, we do it again. You see a pattern?"

He wiped his mouth with the back of his hand, then let out a thunderous burp that rolled like a storm cloud. The smell that followed was worse than the lake itself.

"What do you say we skip all that fun," the king said, leaning forward, "and you just tell me—"

"Throw us in the lake," Charli interrupted.

The king stopped. His eyes slid toward her. He licked his lips, the sound squelchy and revolting. For a long, drawn-out moment, he just stared. Then he turned his head toward Jelly, brow deeply furrowed.

"I might've misjudged her, Jell-Bell."

Behind him, the cardboard-thin figures began to mutter like dried leaves scraping together. Whatever they were saying, it didn't sound impressed. Eventually, all three shrugged in eerie unison.

"Jelly, hello?" the king called, waving a hand. "What'd you think?"

"About?"

"About... you know." The king waggled his bushy eyebrows. "Don't make me say it, Jelly Roll."

Jelly sighed. Turned in Charli's direction.

"The king needs a queen."

Charli turned to Van, confusion flashing across her face. They didn't understand what was being proposed.

"Wouldn't you like to be queen?" Jelly said, tone flat as pavement. "Every girl wants to be a queen. Imagine, all this could be yours—"

"I'm not going to be queen," Charli said.

"There it is." Jelly's lips curled into a sly grin. "First test... passed."

"What test?"

"A true naughty queen never wants to be queen. That's how we know you're real."

"Well, I don't want to be queen. And I'm definitely not going to be queen."

"Got it. Now for the second test—"

"No. No second test. I'm not—"

"How good are you at eating chocolate?" the king interjected.

"That's not the second test," Jelly muttered. "The second test is the naughty test."

"I don't care what it is," Charli said. "I'm not going to be queen."

"You already passed the first test!" Jelly snapped. "Now if everyone will just—"

"She's not going to be queen!" Van stepped in front of Charli like a shield. "She means it."

"I'm getting a migraine," Jelly muttered.

"Shut up! Everybody shut up!" the king bellowed.

He berated everyone present, including the paper cutout crew who were just standing there doing nothing. Jelly argued it wasn't her fault (which it wasn't), that this always happened when the king fancied someone on a whim and insisted on making her a queen. Which never worked. Never ever.

Van started edging his way along the wall, grabbing Charli to follow. The trees weren't too far away. They could be in them before anyone noticed. What was the king going to do, drive after them?

The plan changed when the king jabbed a stubby finger at Van.

"Throw that one in Fudgy Lake! She stays until she accepts the proposal."

"Proposal?" Charli grabbed Van's arm, holding on tight. "I'd rather swim."

The cardboard figures gasped in unison, a theatrical intake of air that sounded rehearsed. A flurry of high-pitched whistles followed. Some musical, some mocking. They clapped their stiff, papery hands like an overexcited studio audience.

The king grunted, nodding as if their reaction had confirmed a long-held suspicion.

"Soooo," he said, smirking, "you like him, is that it?"

"Of course I do."

Van felt his face heat up, a pulse of embarrassment blooming behind his ears. The darkness did him a favor, hiding the blush that overtook his cheeks. He knew she didn't mean it that way, but still, hearing those words from her sent a small, unexpected warmth through his chest.

The king raised one bushy brow. "So that makes you his queen, then?"

"I'm nobody's queen." Charli's hand tightened on Van's arm. "Van's a good person. Thoughtful. I see how he is at school. How he holds doors open for people. Helps them with homework. He's quiet, and most people don't really notice him. I do, though."

Van stared at the ground, trying to will his heart to slow down. It didn't matter how she meant it. The words were enough. Especially that last part.

"Dude," the king chuckled, rocking back in his throne, "you're so in the friend zone. Like deep, bro. Stings a little, huh? But you, young lady... points deducted. That was way too nice. A naughty queen doesn't talk like that. Disgusting."

He paused, rubbing his chin thoughtfully. "But... points for the friend-zoning."

"Right in his face," Jelly said.

"In his face is how it's done," the king said, snapping his fingers. "String 'em up, make 'em feel it, and then boom. Right into the zone. You've got potential, girl."

"Mad potential," Jelly agreed.

No matter what he said, no matter how long they were stuck here, no matter what kind of throne or test or title he dangled in front of her, she was not becoming queen. Not even if they never made it home. Not even if he locked her in a candy-coated dungeon or crowned her with chocolate truffles.

And anyway, where was the castle? A proper king lived in a castle and none was in sight.

The king slammed his fist onto the armrest with a loud, echoing thud, letting out a wail like a ship's horn. The sound was mournful, absurd, and oddly theatrical. A whale in emotional distress.

From the shadows emerged two wooden puppets. They were rigid, creaking, their joints clicking with each awkward step. They each carried a charcuterie board piled high with chocolate truffles, fudge squares, candy bark, and cocoa-dusted buttons.

They bowed stiffly and set the platters on the king's lap with a care that contrasted disturbingly with their splintered, doll-like limbs. The king waved them forward again, and the puppets obeyed, lifting the trays higher as he dragged his hand through the pile.

With no ceremony at all, he shoveled a grotesque amount of chocolate into his gaping mouth.

The chewing began. Like boots in a swamp.

Van flinched. Charli turned away.

"You're coming to the top of the castle with me; I want you to see the view. There's beauty in darkness."

The king tapped a joystick at the end of his armrest, and with a mechanical hum, his throne sprang to life. It whirred and jerked as it spun around, lurching over scattered debris with all the grace of a runaway dumpster. He grunted in frustration, rocking it forward.

Just before vanishing through the doorway carved into the rock wall, he tossed over his shoulder, "You can take the stairs."

"We're not going up," Van said, loud and firm.

"Good. Because I wasn't talking to you."

"I'm not going," Charli said. "I'll swim all night."

"That's an option," the king replied.

The king coolly drove his weird throne scooter at the opening in the stone wall with his cutout entourage in tow. The heavy door began to swing closed when Van interrupted the exit.

"What are you going to do with the hat?"

The throne screeched to a halt. A moment later, the king's hulking shadow spun around in the doorway, completely blocking the blue-tinged light behind him.

"Not your business." There was a long pause. Then, as if enjoying the attention, he added, "But if you must know... I'll probably use it to make chocolates even more delicious. I'm not sure that's technically possible. But I'll try."

"Is Christmas going to disappear?" Charli asked.

"Who told you that? The Nogster?" the king sneered. "That

goody-goody doesn't know his chocolate from his cake." He waved a lazy, dismissive hand. "I mean, it's technically true. That is the Toymaker's hat you took. And yes, you did steal it. Impressive, honestly."

"But what will happen to Christmas?" Charli asked.

The king's expression changed. Just slightly. The throne creaked as it rolled a few inches out of the doorway, his face flickering in the strange, unnatural blue glow. A cruel smile crept across his lips.

"It won't disappear. Not entirely." He rested his bulk against the side of the throne. "I lie all the time. It's kind of my thing. But this time, I'm telling the truth. Christmas will still exist. It just won't be as... special. But you can't have it all. And to be honest, it's a little selfish to want it all. I do, but I'm King of the Naughty. It's what I do. But you, with your naughty and your nice, you just want more presents and act like you don't."

For the briefest moment, something shifted in his expression. A flicker of doubt. Of regret, maybe. Almost imperceptible. Then it was gone. The silence that followed settled thick around them, heavy with unspoken things.

But it didn't last long.

"I'm heading up." He glanced around the chamber, scowling. "Carl! Carl! Where's Carl? Carl!"

His face flushed a deep, angry purple. The throne rumbled in agitation beneath him.

A heavy door creaked open in the stone wall. Out lumbered a massive figure. Tall, broad, swaying slightly with each step. At first, Van thought it was some kind of troll. Something that looked like a gorilla. Or maybe a trick of the low light. But as it stepped closer, its long arms swinging and its chest puffed under a stretched button-down shirt, Van realized he was wrong.

Carl wasn't like a gorilla. Carl was a gorilla.

A gorilla in ill-fitting clothes.

And a tie. A crooked, wrinkled tie that hung sadly around his thick neck like someone had forced it on him hours ago and he never figured out how to adjust it.

"Carl, I'm heading up to my room, and you're going to toss my naughty friends into Fudgy Lake. But not until I get up there. I want to watch."

Carl gave a slow, thoughtful grunt and pointed at Jelly.

"Not her," the king added. "Unless you want to."

"You're not throwing me in, Carl," Jelly said flatly.

"Whatever. As long as those two go for a swim, I'm peaches. Just wait till I give the signal. Got it?"

"Why not just watch from here?" Van asked.

The king rolled his eyes as if the answer were so obvious it didn't deserve one. He turned back to Carl, grinning with chocolate-stained teeth.

"Now, after you dunk 'em, you fish 'em out and cover them in sprinkles. And I mean cover them. In their ears, between their toes. Everywhere. You got that, Carl? Then, once they're gooey and crusty, bring them up. They'll give me the answer I want or it's splish-splash."

With a satisfied grunt, he spun his throne around, flattening two of the cardboard figures without a second thought. They flailed in silent, awkward flutters, then sprang back up and hurried after him, their limbs clicking and twitching like broken marionettes.

The king rolled through the doorway, already shouting at someone to move before the stone door slammed shut behind him.

THE WALL he vanished into wasn't just a wall. It was part of a tower. Though tower was a generous word. It looked more like a rotting tooth that had burst from the ground, crooked and broken, its blackened stone clawing at the sky.

Van stared up at it, trying to trace its height, but its top vanished into the thick, inky darkness above. It didn't look like it ended. It just kept going.

"You okay?" Charli asked.

Van wasn't okay. He didn't know how to get out of this mess. The dream theory was starting to crumble. Reality was closing around him with giant gorilla arms. Running away was pointless. They had no map, no plan, no sense of the world beyond the circle of gloom that surrounded Fudgy Lake. And worst of all, the air felt like it was closing in.

Something cracked in the forest behind them. A loud, wet snap, like bones under pressure. Massive bones.

Then came a low, guttural sound. Not quite a growl, not quite a voice. It vibrated in the ground beneath their feet.

"Sweet Tooth," Jelly muttered.

"What?" Van asked.

"Nothing." She didn't look at him. Her eyes flicked toward the trees, calculating. "If you're thinking of running... don't."

They couldn't trust anything she said. But something in the way she said that made the hairs on the back of his neck rise. She didn't say it was dangerous. Not directly. But she didn't have to.

The sound came again. Closer this time.

They stood at the foot of the tower, trapped in a world that felt more like a fever dream than reality. A super long never-ending fever dream. It was like time had bent, stretched, and forgotten them. Hopelessness climbed on top of them. And then, without warning, Charli slipped her hand into his.

She didn't say anything. She didn't need to.

He kept his eyes closed, the warmth of her fingers a small comfort in the middle of this nightmare.

For a fleeting moment, he let himself believe they were just two ordinary people, standing there, holding hands in a world that wasn't twisted or cruel. A world where time wasn't broken and monsters didn't smile. A world where they belonged.

But that world wasn't here.

"All right, the royal creeper is up in his room now, peeking out the window," Jelly announced. "Straight ahead, girls and boys. And if you failed geometry, Carl here will be happy to teach you what a straight line is."

Van and Charli said nothing. Their hands remained clasped as they walked forward, one cautious step at a time. The air was thick with caramelized fear and burnt sugar. All around them, shadows twisted like taffy, stretching too long in the flickering light.

Behind them, the tower loomed, jagged and broken. It rose like a dead tooth against the night sky. Some parts glowed faintly, pulsing in and out like the heartbeat of something dying. High above, a few lights winked in and out, too distant to be understood. The king might have been up there, watching. Van no longer cared.

Ahead was a dark, oozing expanse of oily fudge. It shimmered with an unnatural sheen, its surface sluggish and bloated. Alive. Like it was waiting.

Van, strangely, felt a flicker of anticipation. In a world where everything had spiraled beyond his control, the idea of wading into something thick and terrible was almost... comforting. It had rules. Gravity. Viscosity. It would hold him, slow him down, wrap around him like a weighted blanket. It would at least make sense.

Then, from the shadows, something moved. A figure darted in front of them. It landed with a slap on the sticky path, crouched low like it had sprung from a spring-loaded trapdoor. It was barely a foot tall, no more than a sliver of a thing, thin as a cracker.

Van stopped short. So did Charli.

The creature tilted its head. Its body was flat, wafer-thin, with stiff limbs and a paper-like texture. Its eyes were dollops, like chocolate chips half-melted and slightly sunken. It didn't speak. It had been expecting them.

Jelly sighed behind them.

5

"What do we have here?"

The voice belonged to the gingerbread cookie. A classic rendition straight from a child's imagination. A red gumdrop bow tie at his neck. His smile stretched wide, sugar-slick and just a little too eager. His arms and legs were rounded, crisp at the edges, like someone had pressed him from a mold. But when he moved, it wasn't with the snap of baked dough.

He flexed. Bent. Twisted. Not like something baked but like something born.

"Move," Jelly said flatly.

"I've got a feeling these two don't belong here."

"And I've got a feeling Carl can make crumb cake."

The gingerbread man's icing eyes widened, then narrowed again, crinkling at the edges. Still, he didn't leave. Instead, he began skipping beside them, his tiny feet clicking against the gummy stone path like polished buttons.

"You hear how she talks to citizens, kids? A real charmer." He gave Van and Charli a slow, exaggerated once-over. "Let me guess. You two aren't here by choice."

They shook their heads, silent.

"What'd they do, Jelly? Feed a stray dog?" He gave a short, snort-like laugh. "Look, kids, the swim's not bad. Sure, it's sticky. Sure, the sprinkles get everywhere. But is that really the worst thing that's ever happened? The king calls it torture, but honestly? Nobody cares. Like at all."

"Leave, flatbread. Go irritate the nice side."

"Maybe I will. But like... right now you got me curious." He eyed Van and Charli. "What's the deal with the kids?"

"Carl."

Carl, the gorilla enforcer, took a deliberate step forward. His weight made the ground quiver. His dark eyes found the gingerbread man, narrowed slightly. Something close to boredom.

The cookie took a small, careful step backward, hands raised in exaggerated surrender.

"Hey, Carl, buddy. We're friends. Remember that one time I gave you a banana made of licorice? You liked that, remember?"

Carl didn't blink.

"It was Tuesday. You said it was chewy in a good way. That's not nothing."

Still nothing from Carl.

"Look, I know I can be a little much sometimes. But you? You're all muscle, no nonsense. We balance each other. It's like buddy cop energy. I'm the mouth, you're the punch. Classic formula."

Carl exhaled through his nostrils. It was like a furnace breathing.

"Okay. I get it. The king told you to do it. And, let's be honest, you're a bit of an approval junkie. But look at these kids, Carl. They're adorable. Practically shaking."

Van and Charli were absolutely not shaking but did not speak up to correct him.

"I'm just saying maybe don't resort to violence over a conversation. Maybe we give peace a chance. Remember that song? Anybody?"

Carl's pace quickened.

"Or maybe we don't. That's cool, too. Totally fair." The ginger-bread man's voice dropped. "Okay. Wow. That's the face you make before throwing someone into the fudge pit. Very intimidating. Very 'silent-but-deadly.' Love that for you."

Carl lunged.

The cookie yelped, high-pitched and immediate. Leapt backward in a blur of motion, icing flinging from his arms like sweat. He twisted in midair, flipped, and landed on the tip of a candy cane bollard.

"Remember the banana!"

The ground trembled with each thunderous step as he charged, fists clenched, jaw set. But the gingerbread man was already moving, zigzagging in a sugar-fueled blur, impossible to track. His tiny feet left streaks of powdered sugar.

He darted between Van and Charli so fast they flinched, looped around their ankles, leapt up and over Jelly's shoulder, then slipped down the back of her coat. A beat later, he popped out from her sleeve, landing behind her with a smug little bow.

Carl couldn't stop in time. His momentum carried him straight into Jelly. The collision sent her sprawling, frosting streaking across the gummy cobblestones.

The gorilla barely paused. With a growl of frustration, he wheeled around and charged again, giving chase. The gingerbread man? He laughed. Loudly.

"Oh, come on, Carl. This is just embarrassing!"

It was like watching a circus act gone rogue. Carl smashed through gumdrop barrels and licorice arches while the cookie zipped through gaps that barely existed, moving like light and speaking twice as fast. If the king was watching from his high window, he wasn't happy.

The gingerbread man dodged. He danced. He heckled. He ran literal circles.

The best part?

He looked like he could do this all day.

POW!

A sharp crack, a cloud of sugar-dusted smoke, and the gingerbread man vanished.

Jelly stood still, slingshot raised, already sliding another chocolate-covered walnut into the pouch with professional calm. The scent of cocoa and scorched candy hung in the air. As the dust settled, the only thing left was a small, smoking divot in the path. If the gingerbread man's heroics had been short-lived, nobody could say they weren't sweet while they lasted.

"Bro. That was close."

The gingerbread man emerged from the haze like nothing had happened, brushing cookie crumbs from his shoulders and shaking himself off like a powdered spaniel. He pointed to his knee, where a chunk of icing had been blown clean off.

"Look at that. You're good, Jelly. Seriously. That one had intent."

Jelly snapped the slingshot again. Another walnut screamed through the air, ricocheting off the ground and disappearing into a patch of gumweed. But the cookie had already twirled out of reach, his tiny feet skating across the sticky ground, leaving streaks of cinnamon. He weaved, spun, twisted like ribbon candy in a storm, his movements sharp and theatrical.

Every dodge came with flair. Every leap an exclamation point. He even paused mid-cartwheel to wave.

Carl barreled forward, arms wide. The gingerbread man zipped between his legs, slid past Jelly's boots, ricocheted up her back, over her shoulders, and spiraled into the air like a confetti cannon. He landed in a superhero crouch. Followed by a little bow.

It was a game. And he was winning.

But then in the blink of an eye, as he lunged into another showboating spin, Carl shifted. Just a hair. Just enough. The gingerbread man twisted midair—

Carl caught him.

A gasp rippled through the air. The gorilla stood still, hands clamped around the wriggling cookie like a prize he wasn't sure he'd meant to win. His wide eyes stared down at his hands.

Jelly raised her hands in triumph. "Finally."

Low, bubbling sounds worked their way up from Carl's belly, clumsy and unsteady, like something he hadn't done in years. His shoulders rocked. His eyes watered.

He shook once. Then again. And again.

It wasn't joy. It wasn't victory. Something was happening inside his hands.

"Tickle, tickle," came a smug, singsong voice from between Carl's fingers.

"You've got to be kidding me."

Carl wheezed, a strange whimpering chuckle gurgling out of him. His body lurched sideways as he tried to suppress the reaction.

"Right in the palm lines, buddy. You've got very expressive nerves. Left quadrant, prime giggle zone."

Carl looked like a landslide trying not to happen.

"You hear me in there, gingerbread?"

"Loud and clear, Jelly Beer!"

Jelly's eye twitched. "Keep listening. Carl, I want you to crush him. Turn him into flour. And when we drag the boy and girl out of the lake, we'll sprinkle him on top. The king will love it."

Carl stopped giggling. His face changed. Brow creased. Smile faded. He stared down at his hands.

Crush him? Just like that?

Sure, the little guy was a menace. Loud. Impossible to control. But something about flattening him into crumbs didn't sit right. Maybe it was the way he tickled. Maybe it was the licorice banana. Maybe it was the fact that, deep down, the gingerbread man was right.

Carl liked him.

The gingerbread man had always made things interesting.

"Carl," Jelly said again. "The king will be proud."

"You gonna crush me, big guy?" came the muffled voice. "No hard feelings, if you do. But just remember. I still owe you a banana."

Carl looked at her, then at his hands. Like a soldier following an order he didn't understand but would obey anyway.

He raised his hands, slowly, ready to smash them together like twin anvils. Ready to reduce the gingerbread man to dust and memory.

"You might want to check your pocket, Jelly-Do."

"Wait! What did he just say?"

"I think," Van offered, "he said you should check your pocket."

Jelly's eyes narrowed, deep lines bunching at the corners. She didn't trust a single syllable out of that cookie's mouth. But something about the tone set off a deep and immediate alarm inside her gut. He was too calm. Too knowing.

Her thick brows collapsed like storm clouds. She glanced down at her coat. Slowly at first, then with increasing speed, she began patting the wide expanse of fabric stretched over her belly. Her hands slipped into seams, flipped open flaps, unbuttoned hidden layers.

Each pocket she opened and checked revealed nothing. Until the last one. Her fingers slipped into the deepest seam.

And stopped.

Her eyes went wide, panic flashing across her face like lightning across a darkening sky.

"Carl," she said. "Listen to me very closely. Are you listening? I want you to start opening your hands, but" — she jabbed a stubby finger at him — "do not, and I mean do not let that rotten cracker escape."

"Crackers can't go rotten," the gingerbread man called.

"Carl! Do you understand?"

Carl gave a slow, obedient nod.

Jelly exhaled through gritted teeth. Counted down from three. Then gave the signal.

Carl's giant fingers began to unfurl, thick and careful, like petals blooming from a concrete flower. As they spread, the gingerbread man stretched luxuriously, arching his back, rubbing his icing-smeared eyes.

"Ahhh. Gotta say, Carl... very soft hands. You lotion?"

Jelly leaned in. "Where. Is. It."

"Where is what?" Then he patted himself down. "Hmm. Let's see here... No, not there. Not in the gumdrop belt. Ooh—wait."

He reached into a fold of his frosting-streaked vest and produced a small, shining object.

A button.

Not just any button. The same one that had triggered the portal back in the ice room. The one that had dropped Van and Charli at the foot of this rank fortress. The one that had been in Jelly's inner pocket.

Somehow, in the chaos, in the blur of flips, twirls, tickles, and near-annihilation, the gingerbread man had snatched it clean from her.

Jelly's entire body went rigid. Her fists clenched so tightly, they turned from pink to white to pale green.

"Looks like we've got ourselves a good old-fashioned stalemate," the gingerbread man said, twirling the button between two sticky mitts. "And I happen to know just how valuable this little doodad is. I mean, I could march it straight to the Big Bad Wolf's camp, and you know how much he'd give for it."

He gave a low, exaggerated whistle.

"A king's ransom. Easy." His gaze flicked briefly toward Van and Charli. "And you also know how mad the king would be if the wolves got their paws on this little trinket. Pretty sure Carl here would be the one marching you down to Fudgy Lake."

Jelly's nostrils flared. "What do you want?"

"Simple. I take the kids. You get the button back. Nice and clean."

"You know I can't do that."

"Well, you know you can."

"No. I can't."

He flipped the button into the air, caught it, and tucked it into some unseen compartment.

"Guess it'll be an early Christmas for the wolves."

Jelly's face was pale, her usual sour sneer crumbling into something closer to desperation. She had the look of someone trying to hold a collapsing gingerbread house together with a single gumdrop. Her grip tightened around her slingshot, but even she knew there was nothing she could do.

Carl had the gingerbread man in his enormous hands and still couldn't finish the job. And if the cookie decided to make a run for it? Forget it. Carl would trip over his own knuckles before he landed a single paw.

"We're in a real pickle, aren't we, Jelly? I want the kids. You want the button. Anything else you want? 'Cause I just want the kids. Nothing else here for me."

"What?" She turned to Carl. "Listen, thin mint. You ain't getting the kids. Now what else?"

"Thin mint?" The cookie placed a dramatic hand on his chest. "Kids, do I smell like a thin mint to you? Peppermint's a choice, Jelly-Belly. I'm molasses swagger, you know that."

Carl continued to hold him, completely motionless, as though maybe if he stood still long enough, this would all go away.

"Are you suuuuure there's nothing else you want?" the gingerbread man said. "Nothing at all? Like you just want the kids nothing else?"

"What are you talking about? You know I want the—"

"The hat!" Van blurted out. "He's talking about the hat!"

The world seemed to stop. All eyes whipped to Van.

He stood his ground, heart pounding, but his face calm. The gingerbread man gave him a sly, appreciative wink, and Van felt a shift, like something had finally tilted in his favor.

For a moment, he thought: Maybe the king's right. I do belong on the naughty side.

A slow smirk tugged at the corner of his mouth.

"What if I tell you where the hat is?" Van said. "That's what you really want."

"That, and she's going to be queen."

"Yeah, but what do you want more?" Van tilted his head slightly. "I think it's the hat."

Jelly opened her mouth to argue. Her lips pressed tight, her jaw flexing. The silence between words said what she couldn't.

The king wouldn't care about a queen for long. He'd get bored, distracted. But the hat. The hat had legacy. Power. The kind of artifact that earned loyalty and fear.

"I'll tell you right now where it is," Van said. "No tricks, no games."

He glanced at the gingerbread man, who wiggled in Carl's grip like he was getting comfortable.

"If," Van added, "you let us leave with him."

"Ohhh, now that's a sweet deal," the gingerbread man said, whistling low. He rocked back in Carl's hand like he was lounging in a recliner. "I don't know how you're going to turn that down. I mean, really. I just stepped in and got you exactly what you wanted. And Carl here didn't even have to get his hands sticky."

Jelly didn't answer right away. Her eyes darted between Van, the cookie, and the space in her coat where the button used to be.

"If I do this," she said, low and serious, "you're giving me back the button. Right?"

The gingerbread man placed a hand over his nonexistent heart.

"Jelly, please. What kind of cookie do you think I am? Of course you get the button. You give me the kids, I give you the button. And bonus prize... you get the hat. Two-for-one special, Jelly Bear. I don't even know why you're still thinking about it. If the king were here, he'd—"

"All right. All right, all right. It's a deal."

"It's a deal! All right, kids, hands up. Doesn't matter which one. Now, repeat after me," the gingerbread man instructed, lifting his tiny mitt. "I, state your name, promise to hold true to this deal, and should I break that promise, may the Sweet Tooth grind my bones and drink them in a smoothie."

Van stared at him. Charli muttered, "...Grind our bones into a smoothie?"

"You don't want to know. Now do you or don't you? I suggest the first one."

After a beat, they repeated the oath in unison.

"Boom! I smell a deal." The gingerbread man clapped his tiny hands together. "And now, let's get to—"

"Not like that." Jelly cut in. "You do it with the Lily."

If his icing eyes could roll, they would have circled the moon. "With the Lily, with the Lily," he muttered, waving one hand. "You don't trust them?"

"I don't trust them. I don't trust you."

"You have trust issues."

"I have gingerbread issues." Jelly pointed. "You two. Grab a flower."

VAN AND CHARLI didn't move right away. They waited until the gingerbread man gave a resigned nod toward the lake. It wasn't far. But it felt like a hundred.

The shore of the oily fudge lake shimmered like diseased glass, a dark mirror streaked with caramel-colored slime. The air near it was thick and the smell hit them before they took even three steps. A wave of burnt molasses and something fermented clung to them. Sluggish bubbles surfaced, popping with faint wet burps, releasing clouds of something worse than rot.

Flowers grew in a tight cluster at the edge, where the fudge met the gumroot soil. They had thick, lumpy stems and waxy petals the color of old teeth. They didn't sway or flutter. They just sat there. Waiting for prey.

"Ugh," Charli muttered, covering her nose.

Van motioned for her to hang back. He took a shallow breath and stepped closer, one hand over his mouth. The second he reached the lilies, he bent down and yanked one from the ground.

Big mistake.

The moment it was uprooted, something deep and foul was released. It was no longer just burnt sugar and bad fudge. It was road-kill-in-an-outhouse bad. Like moldy eggnog left in the sun.

"Don't drop it!" Jelly barked.

Van gagged, stumbling backward with the flower between two fingers and held as far from his body as possible. His stomach twisted. He thought he might actually vomit.

Charli watched with wide, horrified eyes, backing up two more steps and pinching her nose even tighter.

"Hold it in your right hand," Jelly ordered. "Both of you."

Charli hesitated, then reached out, wincing as the stench burst free. She gagged, nearly knocking it out of Van's hand.

"Hold. Still," Jelly snapped.

The gingerbread man fanned the air. "No one should have to endure this level of flower-based trauma."

"Shut it," Jelly said. "Now do the vow properly."

Van clenched the flower in his right hand, grip firm but careful. The stem was warm and pulsing slightly, like it had its own heartbeat. Worse, the smell was sinking into his pores, curling around his throat like a furry scarf.

Charli gagged, her face twisted in misery. Then, without a word, she reached over and wrapped her fingers around his. Her touch was grounding. For a second, it was almost enough to steady his stomach. *Almost.* The air still reeked like molten garbage pie.

"Both hands on the stem. That's the deal," Jelly barked.

Charli grimaced but obeyed, gripping the brittle stalk alongside Van. The flower crunched slightly, stiff and unyielding, like it had been grown from wires instead of roots.

The gingerbread man, still lounging in Carl's grip, said, "What's your name?"

Charli said: "What's that got to do with—?"

"Just answer. What's your name?"

"...Charli."

Nothing happened.

The lily's reek stayed steady and brutal. The stem didn't move. The gingerbread man's icing grin stretched wider. Like it had no limit. Like it was daring her to understand something she hadn't grasped yet.

"What's your *real* name?"

Charli hesitated. "...Charlotte."

The moment the full name left her lips, the stem gave a violent twitch. It buzzed once in their hands, then snapped limp like a soaked rope noodle. The stench, which had already seemed impossibly foul, doubled down, twisting into something almost supernatural. Like rotted holiday ham left in a sewer.

"Oh, *come on*," Van gagged as the limp flower sagged between their hands.

"Voodoo lilies can't stand the truth," the gingerbread man said. "We're gonna need one more. Sorry, kid." He did *not* sound sorry.

"Seriously?" Van coughed.

"It's called insurance," Jelly said. "Now stop whining. It's just a smell."

Van muttered something under his breath and trudged back toward the lake. He moved like someone being led to a very stupid execution. This time, he didn't even pretend bravery. He just yanked the nearest flower from the ground, held his breath, and ran back before the smell could dig in too deep.

He thrust the new lily toward Charli. She took it with visible disgust, holding it between two fingers like it might bite.

Jelly let them marinate in the flower's curse. "Now you talk. Where's the hat?"

"It's in a car."

"And?"

"Under the driver's seat."

"Aaaaaand?"

"And… that's where it is."

Jelly's eyes narrowed into slits. Her nostrils flared as she glanced toward the castle. In her mind, she could already see the king revving his gilded throne and smashing peppermint chalices against the wall.

"If he finds out you're wasting my time—"

"I *told* you where the hat is. It's the truth. Look."

The voodoo lily in their hands gave a faint tremble. Then drooped like it had been scolded. The stalk went limp. The petals curled in on themselves. And then the smell twisted into one final exhale of foulness before the whole thing collapsed.

Van and Charli dropped it and staggered backward, shaking out their hands like they could fling the stink off their skin.

Jelly growled. Half frustration, half disbelief. She'd been played into a corner. Outwitted by a kid and a cookie. And now the truth sat in front of her, reeking and undeniable.

"Oh no. Oh no, no, no." Jelly cracked with fury. "This isn't the deal!"

"I'm afraid *it is* the deal," the gingerbread man replied. "He told you exactly where the hat is. Voodoo lily confirmed. Magic flower don't lie."

Jelly's face turned beet red. Overboiled-kettle beet red. She stomped once, twice, fists clenched, rage spilling over like a shaken soda can.

"CHEATERS!" she screamed. "You broke the oath!"

But the truth had been spoken. Just not the version she wanted. She'd asked for the location. Van gave it. If she'd wanted GPS coordinates, serial numbers, and sugar-polished floor maps, she should've said so.

"So..." the gingerbread man drawled, brushing imaginary lint from his gumdrop vest, "the kids are mine now. Sorry, not sorry."

Jelly's jaw locked. "Carl, smash—"

But she didn't get to finish. Because the voodoo lily on the ground suddenly twitched. Its wilted petals snapped open in a jolt, stretching unnaturally wide like a mouth that had waited too long to scream. The bulging pistil at the center began to swell like a blister about to burst.

"*YUUUUUUUM!*"

The shriek ripped through the air like a cat being strangled inside a flaming bagpipe. It wasn't just noise. It was sound weaponized. A single, screeching word that hit like a sledgehammer to the inner ear.

Van and Charli clutched their ears. Jelly staggered backward, flailing her arms as if trying to beat the noise out of the sky.

The lily vibrated once more, the sound still echoing like the ghost of a very loud regret. Then suddenly, mercifully, stopped.

Van's ears rang like church bells hit with hammers. Charli looked ready to punch something.

Jelly glared at the gingerbread man. "Go. Take them. I don't care. There's nothing in the deal that says we can't take them back."

"*Touché,*" the gingerbread man said. "Spiteful and flexible. You're growing, Jelly."

"Give me the portal."

"Of course." He turned to Carl. "Big guy, lift me up just a bit? Higher... little higher... there we go."

Carl complied, confused but cooperative, hoisting the cookie above his shoulder like a trophy on display. The gingerbread man extended his arm. The button glinted in his hand, dangling from a thin golden string. It swayed gently, catching the dim light like a baited hook.

"What are you doing?"

"Giving you back the portal," he said, jiggling the string. "Just gotta use it real quick."

"You can't do that."

"The deal never said I *couldn't.*"

"But—"

The gingerbread man's gaze flicked to Van and Charli. And *theirs* flicked right back. They understood. No signal. No words.

As the button's string unraveled like golden taffy, peeling open a sliver of space like curtains parting at showtime, Charli didn't hesitate. She grabbed Van's wrist and dove headfirst into the swirl of dark and gold before the portal fully formed.

Van's boot disappeared last.

The gingerbread man let the button drop into her waiting hand. "*Ta-da.*"

She caught it, fuming. But it was too late. None of them knew where the portal led. Not Van, not Charli, not even the gingerbread man. But one thing was certain.

It was *anywhere* but the Land of Naughty. And that?

That was *nice.*

6

The disorientation hit harder this time. Sharper, more jarring. There was no falling sensation, no slow unraveling of reality. Just *snap*. Like a thread pulled too tight and cut clean through.

They landed in a field of lush, dew-heavy grass. The ground was spongy beneath them, warm and damp. Around them, palms stretched skyward like skeletal fingers. Dense tropical foliage pressed in from all sides, a breathing wall slick with moisture. The air was pungent with the scent of wet earth, overripe fruit, and the sharp metallic tang of an approaching storm.

Van's stomach lurched violently. It felt like stepping off a Tilt-A-Whirl after eating everything at the county fair. His balance buckled, and he slumped to one side, the world tilting and spinning beneath him.

Charli let out a strangled sound, doubling over. She dry heaved into the grass before rolling onto her back, chest rising and falling in uneven bursts.

Above them, the sky boiled. It was a monstrous canvas of swirling purples and bruised grays, clouds curling and uncurling like waves in a roiling sea. A jagged spear of lightning split the sky, followed by a deafening crack that made the trees tremble.

The palm trees were wrapped in holiday lights. Faded, brittle strands flickered weakly in the growing dark. Ornaments dangled from branches like forgotten memories. Most were cracked, sun-bleached, or coated in mildew. They swayed on strings like pendulums marking the time since they'd been hung. The forest looked like it had been decorated for a party that no one showed up to. A celebration long abandoned.

And then the rain began. First a drizzle. Then heavier. Thick drops slapping the leaves in rhythmic bursts that echoed like distant war drums.

Through a break in the foliage, a structure was visible. Something angular and broken, half-swallowed by the jungle. Vines as thick as firehoses choked its crumbling stone walls. A fractured tower jutted above the canopy, black against the storm-wracked sky. Windows glinted with flashes of lightning. Inside them, pale flickers hinted at artificial light. Some glowed steady. Others sputtered and died. Faded garlands still clung to corners of doorframes and shattered balconies. It looked like *Christmas* had come and gone and forgotten.

"We have to move," Van said.

Charli didn't argue. He reached down, grabbed her hand, and helped her up. Together, they sprinted through the downpour, the wind tearing at their clothes and the storm crashing around them.

They ran across the soaked clearing, dodging falling ornaments and slick patches of moss. The path wasn't clear, but instinct pulled them toward the structure. Toward shelter. Toward something that felt like an answer—or maybe just a temporary escape.

By the time they reached the doorway, they were drenched to the bone. Van twisted the handle. He shoved the door open, and they slipped inside just as the sky let loose.

THE AIR INSIDE was thick with dust and time, carrying the scent of old wood and mildewed garland. It wasn't musty so much as heavy, as if the years had settled into the walls and refused to leave.

Their shoes squeaked against faded linoleum, each step unnervingly loud in the silence. The floor, surprisingly, was still intact, the tiles yellowed but unbroken, like a preserved piece of another era.

Murals stretched along the corridor, wrapping the hallway in scenes of holiday cheer, every inch a frozen moment. Children hurled snowballs mid-laugh, their rosy cheeks captured in brushstrokes that somehow still seemed warm. Painted sleds raced down painted hills. A snowman, tall and cheerful, stood at the center of it all, carrot nose pointed forward, top hat slightly askew, coal eyes twinkling with eerie joy.

Above, reindeer soared through a cerulean sky, antlers like branches against the painted clouds, their hooves frozen mid-gallop as if suspended in a race they'd never finish.

The cheer of the murals couldn't mask the hush that filled the hallway. The shadows at the end of the corridor were deep. The doors, each one slightly ajar, seemed too deliberate. Waiting. Watching.

Van and Charli pressed against the cool brick wall and slid to the floor, trembling more from adrenaline than rain. Outside, the storm roared, the wind hammering the building. Rain drummed against the roof in a steady, rapid rhythm. Like footsteps on hollow floors above them.

"The king…" Charli breathed, barely more than a whisper. "What was *that?*"

Van shook his head. He didn't know anymore. He wasn't even sure if it mattered. Whatever this was had lasted too long. Every time he thought they'd wake up, something worse or weirder was around the corner.

"I'm just glad we got out," he muttered.

"Yeah. I really didn't want to be a queen."

That pulled a laugh out of him. Charli snorted. Then she laughed, too. And suddenly, all the pressure that had built inside her cracked open. She doubled over, then flopped backward against the cold tiles, clutching her stomach as laughter burst from her in uncontrollable waves. It wasn't delicate. It was loud and delirious.

"We got saved," she said, "by a cookie."

They howled and couldn't stop. It was catharsis and madness, exhaustion and relief. It was the absurdity of everything, of gingerbread mercenaries, magic buttons, screaming flowers, and a chocolatey kingdom of nonsense. It was the kind of laughter that only comes when there's nothing else left to do.

Their giggles echoed down the hallway, bounced back in strange, warped distortions, like the walls were laughing too. Like something unseen was listening, joining in.

"A gingerbread cookie," Van added.

Charli kicked at his leg with weak protest. "Stop. Stop. I can't—"

But she didn't really want him to. Van was doubled over now, head between his knees, body shaking from the force of it. It felt like his chest might cave in. Like his whole body had been turned up to eleven and couldn't come down.

They barely noticed the way the echoes twisted down the hallway, stretching too long before fading. They didn't hear the rain pound, or how the lightning crackled just a little too close. Maybe it was the relief of being away from Jelly, the king, Fudgy Lake, and those cursed flowers. Maybe it was the comfort of being inside, just the two of them.

For the first time in what felt like forever, they felt safe.

"Run, run, as fast as you can..."

Van stiffened first. Charli was a few beats behind, still catching her breath. At first, she thought Van had said it—his voice had gone rough from laughing too hard. But then she saw his face. He wasn't smiling anymore.

Van pressed a finger to his lips. They held their breath, listening between the raindrops, waiting, hoping it had just been the storm they'd heard.

Something moved. Not in the shadows. Not in the corners.

On the wall.

The mural rippled. Colors swirled, shifting as if the paint were still wet. Shapes twisted. Then, impossibly, they whispered.

Merry, merry...

Van and Charli sprang apart, scrambling backward, their eyes locked on the mural. It had changed. A snowman stood where there had been nothing before. But not one made of soft, powdery snow. This one was gritty. Sandy. The texture was uneven, almost like clumped ash, giving it an eerie, lopsided quality.

It was a Sandman.

They would come to that realization later. Right now, all they could do was stare, hoping their eyes were playing tricks on them.

"I just want to be the first to welcome you," the thing said, rough as windblown grit. "I mean, of all the places you could've gone, you walked right into this building. Almost like it was meant to be."

Its round head swiveled side to side, the grainy edges of its face stretching and reforming with each movement. It wasn't a projection. No light flickered. No screen glowed. It was the mural itself. A living smear of pigment and sand. A dirty snowman with sand-dollar eyes.

"So... the Gingerbread Man, huh?" He looked back and forth. "You're a little freaked out. I get it. You were just in the Land of Naughty, and, well... things weren't looking great. Now you're here, in the middle of one of the worst storms. It's pitch black, and, oh, look at that. Something on the wall is talking to you. I'll give you a minute."

He lifted a twig arm and checked an invisible watch. Then he started pacing along the length of the mural, feet not moving but body grinding across the painted floor. The mural should have ended at the corner, but now it curved along the far wall too, as if the Sandman had extended it by walking.

He made a dramatic move. At least, the mural version of him did. His grainy, sand-speckled body shifted like drifting sediment, rippling across the painted surface as though stirred by wind.

"You can ask me anything, by the way. Because I, my friends, know everything. And I don't just mean little things, like where you left your socks or why bananas go brown the moment you think about eating them. No, no, no. I mean everything. Like you wouldn't believe it everything. Like hold onto your brains because they might just explode everything."

He mimed an explosion, sticks bursting outward, then brushed imaginary dust from his shoulders. His sand-dollar eyes shifted between Van and Charli.

"So," he said. "Questions?"

"Where are we?" Van said, feeling like he'd asked that a thousand times.

"Ah, yes! That!" The Sandman clapped. "You're on an island."

They waited. He didn't elaborate. "What island?"

"This island."

"Where is this island?"

"In the ocean," he replied, beaming. Then, with a thoughtful nod, added, "Well, technically not in the ocean. More like... surrounded by it."

"Okay." Van turned to Charli. "Your turn."

"What's the island called?" she said.

"Ohhh, you mean like a name! Yes, yes, of course. It's called... The Island. Capital I."

He puffed up, clearly impressed with himself, like someone who had just answered a riddle and expected applause. Van, for his part, recognized this kind of answer. It was exactly the sort of vague nonsense he used to dodge questions about the hat.

"Maybe we should start from the beginning."

She didn't mean just here. She meant their beginning. The Christmas party. The glasses. Everything that had led them here. Maybe saying it out loud would help her understand it. Maybe it would stitch the pieces together.

"No need for that," he said. "I know how you got here. You found the glasses. It was a Christmas party, mostly your friends." He pointed a twig at Charli. "Well, actually, all your friends. Van's a little shy."

"I'm not—"

"Oh, buddy, you are," the Sandman said. "You totally are. In fact," he turned to Charli, "he was probably going to bail on your beanbag party. But then you brought out the blades."

"Blades?" Charli echoed.

The Sandman nodded. "The peppermint blades."

The Sandman reached behind his back and pulled out a sleek, dark pair of glasses, identical to the ones from the box in Charli's dad's closet. He held them delicately between his twig fingers and slipped them over his sand-dollar eyes. The lenses clicked softly into place. He rocked his head side to side, like he was tuning an invisible signal.

"You figured these were virtual, right? I mean, that's exactly what they look like." He raised a stick-thin finger. "Only... they weren't quite as virtual as you thought."

"What do you mean?" Van asked.

"What do you mean, *what do you mean*?"

"You're saying they weren't virtual?"

"Uh, yeah. You went there, kid. You went to the Toymaker's Workshop." He gave Charli an exaggerated shrug. "It's like he's hearing this for the first time."

Van's stomach twisted. He'd assumed that what they'd experienced was just an advanced VR experience. Total immersion, next-gen tech. That was the whole point of the blades. A better headset. A more convincing illusion.

"That's impossible," he said, shaking his head.

"So where are you now?" The sand dollars waggled. "Tell me something. Do you know how your phone works?"

"What?"

"Your phone. The circuits. The frequencies. The magic little invisible waves that let you text someone across the world in your pajamas. You understand how all that actually works?"

Van wasn't following. Neither was Charli.

"Didn't think so," the Sandman said. "And guess what? I don't know how the blades work. I just know when you put them on, *poof*. You went somewhere."

It made no sense. None of it did.

"So, rumor has it," the Sandman said, grinding back and forth across the painted wall, "you two stumbled into the Toymaker's

Workshop. Not the big one, mind you. Just a little outpost tucked into a pocket of the North Pole. Handy for overflow and special orders. Busy time of year and all."

He waved a twiggy hand like he was shooing away smoke.

"So anyway, she gets called away. Emergency. Probably a reindeer fire or a rogue nutcracker. Happens more than you'd think. And then —boom. There you two were. A couple of cold little trespassers, swiping the hat and running for the hills."

"We didn't steal it," Charli said.

"Ehhhh... you kinda did. Which is why you ended up in Naughtyland."

Van started pacing. Ten steps forward. Ten steps back. His socks squished inside his shoes. The squeak echoed off the walls each time he pivoted. The hallway felt tighter now, like it was narrowing inch by inch.

The rain had let up, but it was still falling hard enough that neither of them was eager to step outside again. The downpour pounded steadily against the roof, louder now that everything else had gone quiet.

At least the Sandman hadn't asked Charli to be his queen. That had to count for something.

"So you're saying," Van began slowly, rubbing a hand over his face, "that the glasses physically transported us to the North Pole?"

"That's exactly what I'm saying," the Sandman replied.

"But how? How would our bodies go through the glasses?"

The Sandman clicked his twig fingers like a game show buzzer. "Ding ding ding! And there it is! The big one. The mystery. How did a couple of unsuspecting kids slide right through reality like butter on a hot skillet? Want to hear my theory?"

Charli glanced at Van. *Theory* wasn't a comforting word.

"I said you went there," the Sandman continued. "Not your body. Get it? You're not your body. You're something else. You're an awareness. A presence. A spark. Whatever word you want to use. I mean, look at me." He gestured to his grainy form. "I don't have a body, and yet, bam, here I am. And fun fact: I can be here and over there almost instantly. Why? Because I'm not a body. I'm something else. See what I'm getting at?"

"Okay... but when we were in that workshop, we had bodies," Charli said. "We had hands. We could touch things. And if it wasn't our actual bodies, then how did the hat end up in Van's pocket?"

"Huh. That's a solid point." He scratched the bottom half of his round head, sending a light cascade of grit to the floor. "So either this is one giant plot hole... or it's one of those 'how does your phone work' situations. All I know is, the hat's gone because you took it. And they're looking for it. And they're looking for you."

"So what, you're saying the elf came for us in the café, and we were magically transported through some gift box in a pantry to the actual North Pole?" Van said.

"That's pretty much it."

His brain felt like it was short-circuiting. "That was the real North Pole?"

"It wasn't a fake one, kid. When you went there, you went all the way. And guess what? They noticed."

"Who?"

The Sandman's tone shifted. Calm. Serious. "I think you know."

The silence returned. Heavier now. The storm outside seemed to fade beneath the weight of his words.

"Look," the Sandman said, "I don't know why you keep running. They're going to catch you. We're talking about elves, kid. And not the jingle-bell kind you're thinking of. These guys are light-years ahead of the human race. Tech, time, memory, and everything. How they haven't caught you yet?" He shook his head, sand spilling like dust from a collapsing statue. "That's a Christmas miracle."

Van exhaled slowly, the situation sinking in. They weren't just lost anymore. They were on the run. His head spun. Vertigo crept in. And out of everything, the insane journey, the impossible logic, the sheer madness of it all, he found himself asking the strangest question.

"You're saying Santa Claus is real?"

"That's your takeaway?" The Sandman could barely speak between chuckles. "After everything you've been through, that's what's blowing your mind? *Is Santa Claus real*—oh, man. I mean, I don't even know how to answer that. Seriously. You're gonna pop my midsection with laughter. Wooooo... oh."

The Sandman collapsed, laughing so hard the mural beneath him seemed to ripple. He wiped a nonexistent tear from his sand-dollar eye.

"Think about it. You were at the North Pole. Then Candyland. And not the nice side, either. And after all that, you want to know if Santa Claus is real?"

"Candyland?" Charli asked.

The Sandman rolled over and pushed himself up. He pulled a tattered handkerchief from behind his back and blew his nose. Sand and dust sprayed everywhere. He tucked it away and, after a final wheeze, nodded.

"Candyland, yeah."

"Like the game?"

"What game?"

"You know, the board game. With gumdrop roads and pepper-mint forests?"

"No idea what you're talking about. But I do know there's a Naughty side and a Nice side. And trust me, not a lot of people come back from where you were. Once King Chocolate gets ahold of you? Goodnight. I'm shocked he didn't make you his queen."

The Sandman tapped his chin, his eyes distant, as if caught in memory. A flicker of something close to nostalgia crossed his gritty face.

"But then old G-Man cut you loose," he said. "And here you are. Lucky you."

Lucky was not the word that came to mind. Wet, cold, and exhausted. Hunted. Disoriented. Yes. But not lucky.

Charli exhaled sharply, half a laugh, half a shiver. "Well... yeah. We kind of were."

"Because let's be honest," the Sandman said. "This is way too real to be a dream. And you know it."

That fragile hope, that maybe they were still in the café, that this was all some intense hallucination, frayed apart in an instant. Slipped away like a thread yanked loose from the edge of something unraveling.

This was real. This was happening.

"We're never going to be the same after this," Van whispered.

"Yeah, probably not," the Sandman replied, oddly detached. "Trauma's a heck of a souvenir."

"If we're not dreaming... then how do we get home?" Charli said.

The Sandman shrugged. "I can't tell the future. But if you really wanted to go home, why didn't you just tell them where the hat is? It really isn't that hard."

Why hadn't he? The question struck deep, landing hard. Regret settled like a fist in his stomach. *If I had known this was going to happen...*

"What do we do now?" he asked.

"Well, they're going to come for you. That's a given. Everyone knows what you've been up to, where you've been. We all know what the gingerman did. I do, anyway. Pretty sure the elves do, too."

"Wait a second," Charli cut in. "How do you know about the gingerbread man?"

Van's heart thudded faster. She was right. How *did* he know?

The Sandman grinned like a magician.

"How do you think Santa Claus keeps tabs on everyone? You think he's peeking out from behind curtains all year? Watching in real time like some holiday stalker? Nah. This is more subtle. It's like... pollen. Just little specks floating around everywhere."

One of his sand-dollar eyes vanished for a moment, in a sort of strange wink.

"To be honest, I don't really know how it works. But I'm plugged in. I get updates. Little whispers. So yeah, I kinda know what's going on."

Lookies. Jelly had shown them the dusty motes of tattletales. He remembered them swirling near Nog, drifting in the halls of King Chocolate's castle. That's how Jelly knew. That's how she tricked us.

"So we're being watched?" Charli asked.

"You could say it's the universe's way of keeping tabs. So if you want to keep running, just remember—someone's always watching."

"By someone," Charli said, "you mean Santa."

The Sandman shrugged. "He knows when you've been bad or good..."

"They're coming for us?" Van asked.

"They're definitely coming for you."

"Then fine. Let them come. We'll go back to the North Pole, tell them where the hat is, and go home." He looked at Charli. "Right?"

Charli nodded. "Yeah. Nog was nice."

They had nothing to hide anymore. Besides, the truth would send them home. Or wake them up. Either way, this nightmare would end.

"Except..." the Sandman said, raising a twig finger. "They're not the only ones who know where you are." He let that hang for a beat. "Someone still wants a queen, if you catch my drift."

Van let out a long breath and leaned against the cold stone wall. This was getting old. Fast. An endless web. Pretty soon they were going to bump into a spider. And the way things were going, a very big one named Paul or Henry.

Charli stood beside him, her head bumping softly against the wall as she exhaled, worn thin.

"What if the elves get here first?" Van said.

"Well, if you give them the hat, you're going home. They'll put you to sleep, scrub your memory, and send you off. Sure, traces of everything that happened will linger, but only as dreams. Like when kids catch Santa in the act. They feel memories more than they remember them. It's kinda like that. But you'll be okay. Probably."

"Probably? What does that mean?" Van asked.

"It means probably. Because sorta remembering things? That can feel like a burden when you grow up. It's not a perfect system. But they can't have anyone catching Santa in the act and remembering it." The Sandman shrugged. "I'll be honest, I don't really know why. I just know the rules."

Van's head swam, trying to grasp the shape of this world and its logic. Memory wipes. Dream traces. Magic surveillance networks.

Rules that no one seemed to fully understand—not even the people, or elves, or whatever Sandy was.

"All right," Van said. "And what if we don't give them the hat back?"

"Why would you do that?"

"What if we can't find it? What if it's already gone? Like I didn't lock the car door. Someone could've taken it."

"Who would steal an elf hat?"

"I don't know!" Van snapped. *I did. Accidentally.*

A beat of silence. Then the Sandman said, gently this time, "Well... if they don't get it back, and you're the one who took it, they'll put you on trial."

"Trial?"

"It's technically not a trial. But it's totally a trial."

"But I didn't even know the hat was real! We thought it was a game. They have to know that."

The Sandman offered another shrug. "You took the hat. Soooo..."

A jagged bolt of lightning split the sky, blue-white light flashing from open doorways. A thunderclap rattled the walls. Outside, the rain still pounded the roof, though it had started to ease. The storm was tiring, but it wasn't done.

"Is there any way we can hide?" Charli asked. "Long enough to think this through? Somewhere the Lookies can't see us?"

"Oh, there's no avoiding them," the Sandman said. "They're everywhere. Probably watching us right now."

"Right now?"

"Yeah. Right now. Although..." He tilted his head, squinting into the dim hallway. "I don't see them here. Huh. Weird. Sometimes the rain messes with them. Like static on an old signal."

"Well... is there anywhere we *can* hide?" Van asked.

The Sandman scratched his chin, sending a faint trickle of grit cascading down his front. "*She'd* have hiding spots, for sure. You'd have to ask her."

"Who?" Van said.

"Oh, right." The Sandman sounded nervous. And wary. "This is her island."

"Who is she? Never mind." Charli leaned forward. "Will she help us?"

"Well... she runs a little hot. But you could ask."

It wasn't reassuring. But it was something, and they had nothing.

Without another word, the Sandman turned and began to slide down the mural wall, limbs disappearing along painted bricks. His body scraped like gravel on concrete as he faded into the background.

Van and Charli stepped forward, following the path the Sandman had revealed. Their shoes squeaked on the slick floor. Turning the corner, he led them down another long hallway. At the end was a wide, dust-streaked window.

Outside, the island stretched before them. Dark and rain-slicked, its forested edges pulsing faintly with hidden lights and restless movement. The land dropped away, revealing a breathtaking panorama of the island.

A dense tropical forest was wild and unruly, interrupted only by scattered structures. Buildings stood defiant against creeping decay. Vines twisted up weathered walls, and rooftops sagged under the weight of time. Yet somehow, strings of festive lights still blinked from the hidden dwellings, casting soft, multicolored glows in the mist. Silver ornaments dangled from tree branches like strange fruit, glinting with raindrops. It was as if the entire island were frozen mid-celebration, caught in a holiday that refused to end.

In the distance, a lone tower pierced the jungle canopy. Its dark silhouette rose like a blade against the storm-churned sky, massive and silent. It loomed like a monument to something long forgotten—or perhaps not forgotten at all.

Their breath fogged the glass, their ghostlike reflections staring back. Outside, a wide grassy field was bathed in a strange sepia hue from the storm's watery light. The air shimmered with uneasy stillness. Unlike the warped, cartoonish absurdity of Candyland or the toy-strewn workshop, this place felt different.

"I don't know where she is," the Sandman said. "Most of the time, she just... wanders. It's her island. She doesn't answer to anyone." He hesitated. "If you do see her, just go slow. Don't startle her. You know?"

"No, we don't. Why don't *you* talk to her?" Charli asked.

The Sandman muttered something under his breath. Then said, "I'm going to be honest with you. She may or may not like me."

"Why? What'd you do?"

He threw up his hands. "She might know about me, or... she might not."

"Wait. You mean she doesn't know you're here?"

"Something like that."

"Great," Van said flatly. "That's awesome."

"Well," the Sandman said, "there *is* someone who might be able to help. Let me check with him. See if he'll talk to her for you. You two stay here."

He pointed toward the window and the rain-slicked grass below. He turned to scoot down the hallway then, as if an afterthought hit him, stopped and turned.

"Oh, and... you might want to step back from the window. Three steps should do it."

Van paused. Then stepped back.

"Two more."

Charli grabbed his sleeve and pulled him the rest of the way.

"Perfect."

The Sandman began scraping his way down the hallway, voice trailing as he went. "Oh, and... merry, merry. Just in case I never see you again."

THE STORM HAD DULLED to a soft hiss, the rain streaking sideways across the glass. The island outside remained still, shrouded in mist and shadow, pulsing with unseen movement.

Eventually, Charli let out a quiet sigh and slid down the wall, arms wrapped loosely around her knees. She collapsed onto the floor with the kind of weariness that had nothing to do with sleep. A moment later, Van joined her.

They stared at the field below, their reflections dim in the glass, ghosts of who they used to be. Whoever might help them was out there, somewhere in the dark. Van leaned his head back against the wall and closed his eyes.

For a fleeting moment, he wished they could just stay like this. No elves. No hat. No island of impossible memories. Just quiet. Charli's warmth beside him was grounding, a familiar weight in a world that felt increasingly untethered. He could hear the soft click, click, click of her picking at her nails.

"I sit behind you in history class," he said.

"I know," she replied. "We're in the same row."

Van smiled. She knew exactly where he sat. Maybe he wasn't as invisible as he'd always thought.

"You don't really talk to anybody," she added.

"No."

He could've said more, explained the awkward lunches, the lonely bus rides, the online usernames that knew him better than most people ever would. But what was the point? Knowing people wasn't the same as being known. And digital friends, even the ones who checked in at two in the morning, couldn't anchor you in a moment like this.

Charli didn't press. She sat quietly beside him. Then she asked, "Are you going to talk to me when this is over?"

Van turned his head, trying to read her face. "What do you mean?"

"I mean, when we're back home... are you going to talk to me? Or just stay quiet?"

He paused, then nodded. "Yeah. I will."

She rolled her head against the wall, meeting his eyes. A small smile tugged at her lips. In the distance, lightning flared brief and bright, catching in her eyes before fading back into shadow.

Van leaned his head against the cool stone and closed his eyes again, letting the hush fill the space between them. The thought of returning to that dull classroom, the white walls and buzzing lights, the forgotten assignments, felt different now.

"Do you think we can trust him?" Charli asked.

"You mean, can we trust a painting of a Sandman?" Van chuckled. "I don't see why not."

The silence that followed wasn't awkward. It was warm. Peaceful in the way that only comes after chaos.

It didn't matter where the Sandman had gone or what he was doing. Maybe he was summoning elves. Maybe he was making the whole thing up. Maybe he was just wandering through someone else's dream. Or maybe he was never real in the first place and they'd been talking to a wall.

None of it changed the truth pressing down on Van's body. His limbs were heavy. His breath slowed. His eyelids felt like manhole covers.

And for the first time in a long time, he didn't fight it.

"Is he sleeping?"

Van forced his eyes open. The Sandman was wedged between him and Charli, his round, sand-dollar eyes hovering inches from Van's face.

"You snore," the Sandman said.

Van blinked, disoriented. His voice came out hoarse and thick with sleep. "Did you find a hiding place?"

"Well, he was sleeping," the Sandman replied. "And I'm not supposed to wake him up. So I came back down here and listened to you two." He tilted his head, studying them. "It's... kind of interesting, watching you both. The way you act together. It's sweet."

"You were eavesdropping?" Charli said.

"It's what I do."

He didn't elaborate. Just sat there, grinning like a sand-covered Buddha, sand dollars ping-ponging between them with cheerful curiosity.

"So, you're going to tell us to just wait," Charli guessed.

"Pretty much, yeah."

The hallway, dim and quiet, felt wrapped in stillness. There was no rush of footsteps, no threat pushing them forward. Just rain on glass, shadows on stone, and the muted company of someone made of sand.

Every so often, the Sandman let out a long, slow sigh. A sound like the wind dragging over dunes. Somehow, it fit.

Charli leaned her head back and stared at the ceiling. "So... Santa Claus is real?"

The Sandman sighed again. "You already asked that."

"You never answered it."

"Yes, he's real. Totally real. I can't believe we're still on this."

"Well, if he's real, how does he live at the North Pole and nobody ever sees him? That kind of thing was believable a couple hundred years ago, but now? We've got satellites. Drones. Live-streaming penguins. We can see everything. How does someone live up there with a city of elves and nobody notices?"

"Technology, sister," the Sandman said with a shrug. "It's what they do."

"And he delivers presents on Christmas, right?"

"Uh, yeah. Do you not get—?"

"Well, then how does he get around the world in one night?" she pressed. "If you do the math, that's, like, billions of houses. Even if he spent one second at each stop, that's more seconds than there are in a night."

"Yeah, well... technology." He shrugged again, like that answered everything. "Look, I don't know how magicians do card tricks, either."

"Okay, then explain the flying reindeer. Of all the animals that could fly, it's reindeer pulling his sleigh. You're telling me that's real?"

"Yeah, pretty wild, right?"

"And how does he make all the toys? Seven billion people. That's at least seven billion gifts. There'd be a mountain of toys up there. I may have gotten a C in physics, but that's impossible."

"I never said it made sense. I just said it's real. You're thinking like a human. Santa doesn't work the way you think he works. None of this does."

He paused, letting that settle.

"See, you're here." He tapped the ground. "And then there's... them. The ones who made the rules. The ones who keep time from unraveling and dreams from leaking into the universe. And somewhere between them and you is Santa. Just a guy trying to keep the balance. That's his job."

He waved his arms.

"Reindeer, time loops, delivery routes, toy duplication. Whatever it takes. You don't need to understand it. You just need to accept that somehow, against every odd in the universe, it works."

A very long pause lingered. Van stared at him, wide-eyed. Charli narrowed her gaze.

"That," she said, "was the most non-answer I've ever heard."

"Thank you," the Sandman said, beaming. "And you got a C-minus in physics. All I know is this: Santa Claus travels the world, pulled by flying reindeer, delivering presents to everyone. Why's that so hard to believe?"

He wasn't answering the questions, not in a way that made any sense. But somehow, the way he said it made her want to believe it. Like he knew exactly how to sound just plausible enough. If he was some kind of projection, or AI, or enchanted graffiti, maybe that's what he'd been built for.

She ran out of questions. Or was tired of the answers.

"I didn't think Santa was real," Van muttered. His eyes were still closed now.

"Yeah. Most of you don't. That's kind of the problem. But that doesn't stop the big guy. Whether you believe in him or not, he shows up. Christmas spirit doesn't rely on your belief. It's not about you. It lives on with or without it. It's your choice whether or not you feel it."

Van exhaled slowly, shifting in place. "If we get back home... I'll believe."

"Maybe. Maybe not," the Sandman said, quieter this time. "Doesn't matter."

"No, I'm serious." Van opened his eyes and sat up a little. "I will."

"Me too," Charli added. "I'll believe."

"It doesn't matter," the Sandman repeated. "If you get home... I mean, when you get home... you won't really remember any of this."

"You were serious about that?"

"You can't remember. Humanity's not ready. Not for this stuff. No offense, you're still kind of babies. And babies don't get access to elf tech."

All the things they'd survived. The confusion. The fear. And now, to learn that it would all be swept away like a dream? Just flashes and feelings? No proof. Just the haunting sense that something had happened.

Charli had her eyes closed again. Maybe trying to rest. Maybe just pretending. He didn't want to ask. Didn't want to say what he was thinking.

He didn't want to forget this part.

"Hey," the Sandman offered after a long pause. "You want a story? I'm a pretty good storyteller."

"Not really," Van muttered.

The Sandman's face drooped slightly.

They sat together in a still, fragile peace. Trading quiet glances. Watching the jungle sway with the storm's retreat. The wind had settled. The island breathed slower now. The rain tapped gently on the leaves and glass, a steady rhythm that blurred the line between seconds and thoughts.

Above them, the clouds remained thick. Dark. They swirled overhead like the sky was stirring in its sleep, a single eye twitching in a dream it hadn't finished yet. The world felt like it was waiting.

For what, none of them knew.

"Van," Charli whispered.

He had only closed his eyes for a second. Maybe two. It didn't feel like any time had passed. But now she was there, close beside him, pressed against the wall, her breath warm against his cheek.

Charli pointed toward the window, her finger steady, unmoving. The rain had stopped, but the sky was still bruised and restless, cloaked in dark, heaving clouds. Lightning flickered far off in the distance, casting the island in momentary flashes of white-blue light. Thunder grumbled like something buried, something that hadn't yet decided to wake.

Van's mind was fogged with sleep. He followed her gaze out across the field.

The Sandman had been vague about the woman who owned this island. But now, something twisted in Van's stomach. Not fear exactly. More like gravity shifting.

Then came another flash of lightning. This time, he saw her.

She was on the far side of the clearing, a lone figure moving through the field. Not rushing. Just walking. Steady. Intentional.

Van sat up straighter, heart tapping a faster rhythm. Charli tightened her grip on his arm, her face close to his shoulder as she leaned forward, both of them drawn to the glass. He rubbed his eyes. Blinked again. She was hard to see. Just a shadow in a cloak. A shape wrapped in storm-colored fabric.

Mist or steam drifted around her feet, swirling with a will of its own. It didn't rise naturally. It coiled, reached, curled upward in slow, deliberate tendrils, blurring her edges. As if she were part dream. As if the air itself wasn't sure whether or not to hold her in place.

Around her, the atmosphere shimmered. A rippling distortion, like heat waves off asphalt. Like the space around her couldn't settle.

"The Sandman said the boy was awake," Charli whispered. "He was going to talk to her for us."

Van nodded slowly, not looking away. The figure moved with that same calm pace, never hurrying, her shape sometimes vanishing in the mist, only to reappear again like a glitch in space. She wasn't looking for them. She wasn't looking at anything.

But still he couldn't shake the feeling she knew.

Even if they knew how to get to her, they wouldn't reach her before she walked back into the forest. And if they did... *She runs a little hot.*

"Let's wait until he gets back," Van said.

The figure seemed to move outside of time. Each step deliberate. Each moment stretched like taffy. The mist grew thicker, heavier, until she was almost indistinguishable from it. More shadow than person. More presence than shape.

A soft drizzle began to fall again, gentle and silver, blurring the clearing in translucent haze. But it didn't touch her. It slid off the air around her, repelled like she carried her own invisible barrier. She moved to the edge of the jungle, toward the path leading to the tower, never once turning back. Just before the foliage swallowed her—

Something slammed into the grass below.

The impact shook the window in its frame. Van and Charli flinched as a deep thud rippled across the clearing.

Birds scattered from the trees. A low, vibrating hum rolled through the earth. Then silence full of warning.

Smoke rose in a thin column where something had landed. Charred edges curled around scorched grass, steam rising from a small crater just yards from where the cloaked woman had stood.

Whatever it was, it hadn't come from the ground. It had fallen.

A low, guttural roar rolled through the field. Van and Charli moved away from the window, every nerve flaring with primal warning. They couldn't see it clearly—just a massive, shifting shape in the fog and dim light. But it was moving. The way a predator moves when there's no rush.

Van and Charli didn't move. Didn't breathe.

A jagged bolt of lightning slashed the sky. For a single, frozen second, the creature was illuminated.

It was enormous. Towering. A shape twisted between a moose and something more. Antlers stretched out like gnarled branches. Its fur was thick and dark, soaked and matted. It lifted its head like a weight, like a wrecking ball. Inhaled, drawing in the rain-damp air, and let loose a deep, gurgling, resonant moan that wasn't quite a growl, wasn't quite a roar. It was something else. Something that made Van's stomach seize. The noise came from deep inside, as though it carried echoes from some frozen, older place.

Charli's hand gripped Van like a vise. He clenched back, matching her tension. That sound didn't belong to anything in their world.

"What is that?" Charli whispered.

The creature had fallen like a meteor. It moved with intent, sweeping its massive muzzle side to side, sniffing. Searching. And then, it stopped.

It lifted its head and looked directly at them.

Van didn't need to move to know it had locked on. The weight of its gaze hit like cold iron, pinning him to the floor. He couldn't look away. Couldn't breathe. Until instinct finally overrode everything else.

He and Charli slid backward into the dark, low and silent. Each step was weightless, but their hearts thundered. The hallway swallowed them quickly, but even in the dark, there was no hiding. Whatever was out there could smell them. Through walls. Through rain.

Escape was not an option. The Sandman had warned them. Van's mind clung to one single question:

Who found us first?

His answer stood waiting in the hallway.

THREE FIGURES BLOCKED THE CORRIDOR. Still. Silent.

Even in the low light, their shapes were impossible to mistake. Short, wide silhouettes, each about the size of a child. Their outlines almost comical... until you looked too long. Then the strangeness bled through. The proportions were off. Their arms hung low. Their necks were too short. Their heads moved slow. Smooth.

They didn't speak. Didn't step forward. They simply stood there, like a blockade made of breathless flesh and watching eyes. Waiting.

"Good news!"

From behind, there was a soft grinding whisper. The Sandman slid into view, scraping along the wall. His sand dollar eyes scanned their pale faces, then darted to the unmoving trio ahead.

"Never mind," he whispered.

The elves began to move. Their steps were slow.

Scrape... scrape... scrape...

Their feet dragged across the floor like sandpaper grinding over varnish. Every step sent a jolt through Van's spine. The sound wasn't loud, but it was wrong—mechanical and organic at once.

Van and Charli backed up until the cold glass met their shoulders. The window was unyielding. In the field below, the enormous reindeer still watched. But not just any reindeer. It was prehistoric, mythic. Muscles shifted beneath its soaked hide like plates of stone grinding together. Its breath poured from its nostrils in thick, curling clouds, fogging the air like steam from a fractured volcano.

Everything stopped. For a breath. For a blink. Then, with terrifying grace, the reindeer crouched low. And leapt.

It rocketed into the air like it had never belonged to the ground at all. It vanished into the clouds above, swallowed by the storm.

"What do they want?" Charli said.

"I think you know what they want," the Sandman said quietly.

"Is it the hat?" Van asked. "I'll tell you where it is."

The elves halted just outside the halo of light. They were identical. Smooth faces. Expressions carved from marble. Unreadable. Their hair was perfectly braided, each in the exact same way, hanging over their shoulders in mirrored precision. They looked less like people and more like dolls built to enforce rules no one remembered writing.

"Well," the Sandman said, "that explains how they found you so fast."

"What?" Van said.

"You've never heard of the triplets." The Sandman gave a dry chuckle. "There's no Christmas carol about them. Dane, Deke, and Duke. Doesn't exactly sing, right? No sleigh bells. No cocoa. But when something needs doing..." He trailed off, sand dollar eyes shifting toward the trio. "They get it done."

The triplets didn't move.

"They're just going to stand there?" Charli asked.

"They want to know where the hat is," the Sandman said flatly. "Surprise."

"It's under the seat of my car," Van blurted. "Under the driver's seat. I can tell you what the car looks like. Where it's parked. Everything."

One of the elves moved instantly. No warning. No wind-up. It pivoted with unnatural smoothness and shot down the hallway, its strange gait making a soft scratch-scratch sound. The noise echoed weirdly, bouncing between the walls like it didn't want to leave.

The other two didn't move. They just stood there, staring. Those mirrored eyes locked onto Van and Charli. Like they were evidence.

"Is he going to get it?" Van asked.

"Yep," the Sandman said. "It might take a spell, though."

"Why?"

"It's still daylight where you're from. You know, where you left the hat."

"So?" Van said.

The Sandman turned to him slowly. His eyes, for once, weren't amused. "How many elves you see walking around during the day? Or night?"

"We saw one in the café. When Nog tricked us."

"Well, touché. But they aren't Nog. Or careless."

"You can take us home, right?" Charli turned her gaze to the elves, searching their blank faces for any flicker of understanding.

They didn't blink. Didn't tilt their heads.

"Did they hear me?" she pressed.

For a moment, the Sandman was still as paint. A smear of color glued to the wall.

Van felt a sudden twist in his gut. Cold and sharp. A terrible doubt whispered to him, questioning if they'd imagined the Sandman. But then, with a slow grind of gravel, the Sandman stirred. The usual lilt in his voice was gone. Something in him had shifted.

"Yeah, but..." he said, "they're not here to take you home."

One of the elves stepped forward, reached into his coat, and produced a small green box with a red ribbon. He placed it gently on the floor in front of them. No ceremony. No glowing magic.

Van and Charli knew that box. Deep green wrapping. Crisp, almost metallic ribbon.

The elf removed the lid. Then stepped back.

Nothing happened. No swirling portal. No flash of light. Just a box. This one small enough to hold a golf ball.

The elves linked hands with one another. Then, with their free hands, they extended toward Van and Charli. Palms up. Fingers outstretched.

"Let me guess," Van said. "We're going back to the North Pole."

"You're catching on," the Sandman murmured, gesturing toward the box. "The way these things work, you can't just force someone through a portal. You have to choose to go. Like when you opened that box in the pantry. Nobody made you do it."

"Nog tricked us," Van muttered.

"He placed it on the floor. You opened it. Not exactly a trick, but point taken." He nodded toward the elves. "This is more of a gesture. A polite one. If you join hands, you go together. They don't have to do it this way. Could've just thrown you on Ronin's back and hoped for the best."

"Ronin?"

"Big scary reindeer. The one who turned the field into a crater?"

"Oh my God," Charli muttered, dragging a hand down her face. "Is this ever going to end?"

"Once they've got the hat? Sure. You'll wake up at home. Bit of fog, light headache. Maybe an irrational craving for gingerbread. But you'll feel good about it. That's the important part." He gave them a long look. "Right now, though... you should probably go with them. In case it hasn't sunk in yet, that hat is important."

"Okay," she said quietly. "Okay."

Van exhaled. Charli reached out and laced her fingers through his. Her hand was warm. A little damp from fear or rain, he couldn't tell.

What if they didn't cooperate? What if this was a trick? What if Ronin was waiting on the roof, antlers gleaming in the rain?

It didn't really matter. Either way, they were going back to the North Pole.

With a final breath, he reached out. The elf's hand was small but strong. Cool and steady.

As soon as their hands connected, completing the circle, a column of brilliant white light shot up from the box. It wasn't just light. It was a sensation. A frequency that hummed through their bones, vibrating everything loose.

Snowflakes spiraled upward, caught in an invisible wind. They twisted and danced around them, impossibly slow and impossibly fast all at once.

The light was blinding. It passed through Van like warmth in winter, burning away everything heavy, everything scared, everything small. It felt like something inside him was dissolving. Not painfully. Almost... peacefully.

"Bye, kids!"

Through the haze, Van caught a glimpse of the Sandman, stick-thin arm raised in farewell, waving like someone sending off a cruise ship from shore. The walls behind him stretched and unraveled. The colors ran like ink in rainwater, blending into a swirl of white and silver and gray.

He hoped he'd remember the strange little mural who talked too much and helped when it counted. A little annoying. A little wise. Mostly kind.

There were a lot of things Van didn't want to forget. But as the light wrapped around him, pulling him inward like a breath drawn deep into the sky, he felt the memories begin to loosen. Like feathers unthreading from a pillow. One by one.

He held Charli tighter. Just in case they could remember each other.

7

They were met with a blast of bitter cold and a sky so thick with stars it looked painted. It didn't seem possible, that many stars in one sky. They spilled across the heavens in wild constellations, dazzling and endless, like the night had been split open just to show them what was hiding behind it. Van had never seen anything so beautiful. So impossible.

And the cold. It hit like a wall of ice. It stole the breath from his lungs, made his eyes water, numbed his fingertips through the mittens he didn't even remember putting on.

"Come along. Come, come."

The voice was soft. Gentle and caring. Van couldn't tell where it came from. His head still reeled from squeezing through the gift box. His balance wobbled, vision shimmering. The ground beneath him was a flawless sheet of ice, stretching in every direction.

Two of the triplets were already gliding away, smooth and silent on bare feet. They didn't look back. Didn't slow. They moved in absolute sync, drifting like shadows carved from snow. Then, without warning, the ice split open beneath them. No splash. No ripple. One second they were there. The next, gone.

Van stared at the spot where they vanished, blinking through the sting of cold, struggling to understand. Before he could speak, hands were on him, dressing him like a mannequin. Arms shoved into a thick wool coat. A scarf wrapped snugly around his neck. A knit cap pulled low over his ears, nearly blinding him. Leathery mittens slipped back onto his hands, warm and impossibly soft inside.

"Welcome back, boys and girls."

Nog stood on a step ladder, adjusting his gloves with practiced ease. Next to him, another elf stood on a matching ladder, fingers dancing over Charli's coat buttons, cinching them tight up to her chin.

"There we go," she said.

She had a long braid and a calmness in her movements that made Van feel, for some reason, safe. Maybe it was the tone of her voice. Or the smile.

"We won't be on the ice long, but you should stay warm until then."

She and Nog climbed down in perfect rhythm, their giant bare feet padding soundlessly on the ice, unfazed by the freezing surface.

"I hope your journey went smoothly," she said. "If your stomach feels unsettled, we've got remedies for that."

"And if you need to be sick," Nog chimed in, sweeping his arm toward the blank, snowy horizon, "there's the snow to do it. No shame in it. Travel can be... a bit rough. Happens to the best of us."

He clapped a mittened hand on the other elf's shoulder.

"This is my wife, Merry," he said proudly. "She's a bit of a miracle worker. Headaches. Heartaches. Travelaches. She'll sort you out."

As if on cue, the icy hush around them began to fill with a song. Rising from the distance, drifting through the cold like warmth through a window. A chorus of voices, hundreds, maybe thousands of them blending into a rich, joyful harmony. It wasn't solemn. It was lively. Full of motion and life and cheer.

Underneath it, a rhythm pulsed. Clack-clack, clack-clack, it went. Like hickory sticks knocking together. It echoed across the ice like a heartbeat.

Van could almost see it: wooden sword fights, friendly duels, a blur of feet and laughter and movement.

As their senses sharpened, Van and Charli turned slowly, taking in the vast, unbroken expanse of ice that stretched to the horizon in all directions. The sheer scale of it was overwhelming. White on white, glowing beneath a night sky bursting with stars.

Not far ahead, a thrumming energy buzzed. A bustling mass of elves moved with perfect coordination. Bunched together like penguins, they passed brightly wrapped gifts from hand to hand, forming a seamless chain that fed into a glistening sleigh the size of a small barn. Each present vanished into a massive red sack at the back, swallowed up like drops falling into the ocean. Gone in an instant, yet never overstuffed.

Just beyond the sleigh, the source of the rhythmic clatter revealed itself. Dozens of reindeer chased each other across the ice in playful bursts. They darted and dodged, rearing back and kicking flurries of snow into the air. Their hooves drummed against the ice like a symphony of drums. Some leapt so high they seemed to hover, suspended midair like balloons caught in an invisible wind, their antlers etched against the starlit sky.

Though the entire scene played out at a distance, Van and Charli felt a shift. A subtle pause. A ripple through the song. Movement slowed. Heads turned.

Wrapped in thick winter gear, standing out like giants in a sea of small, efficient hands and bright eyes, Van and Charli were no longer just guests. They were the center of attention.

"Well, yes, welcome back," Merry said, stepping between them and the crowd. "Please accept our sincerest apologies. It was never our intention for you to visit the Naughty side. That was highly irresponsible of my husband."

"It was my fault," Nog admitted, raising a hand sheepishly. "I left them for, what, a minute? It was a very chaotic minute."

"He never should have left you alone," Merry said. "We didn't anticipate something like that happening, but we should have been more cautious. Especially with the Toymaker's hat at stake." She shook her head. "And we certainly didn't mean to put you through so many... unexpected experiences. Please, truly, accept our apologies."

Van nodded stiffly, his face half-frozen. The cold gnawed at his skin, biting through the exposed edges around his scarf and hat. Ice crystals had formed on the fine hairs above his lip. Even buried under layers of winter gear, the cold had settled deep in his bones.

"Nog!" Merry snapped, elbowing her husband. "Did you turn the heaters on? They're not accustomed to this climate!"

Nog smacked his forehead with both hands. "Oh! No, I—right! Sorry! Sorry sorry sorry!"

He fumbled with something hidden in the folds of his coat. A moment later, warmth bloomed through their clothing. A subtle glow from inside the seams. The heat spread like a rising tide down their sleeves, through their gloves, into the soles of their boots. Within seconds, Van and Charli were warm again. Not just warm, but toasty. Their breath no longer came out in shudders.

Beyond them, the elves continued moving gifts into the sleigh, a few of them humming again in harmony. But the sleigh-loading team wasn't made up of elves alone.

Two enormous snowmen stood among them. Broad-shouldered. Towering. Their limbs were thick and powerful, blocky like carved stone. They moved with surprising grace, lifting the heaviest packages with ease. No eyes made of coal. No carrot noses. Just dense, icy features.

They were magnificent. And terrifying. Yet peaceful. Controlled.

The elves around them seemed unfazed, as if this were all routine. Just another day. But many of them, maybe most of them, had paused their work. They weren't humming anymore. Their round, flushed faces turned toward Van and Charli, eyes wide with curiosity. Their expressions expectant.

Like the whole North Pole was waiting to see what the two human kids would do next.

"Don't mind them," Merry said. "Most have never seen a full-grown human before. They're just curious."

Van glanced back at the rows of wide-eyed elves. Fascinated. Like they were watching a rare creature step out of a forest they'd only heard about in stories.

"Are we going home?" Charli asked.

"Soon, dear," Merry assured her. "There's just one small thing to take care of first. A bit of housekeeping. Nothing to be nervous about."

Which, of course, only made both of them more nervous. Nothing says worry quite like being told not to.

Van and Charli turned back toward the ice, watching the steady flow of activity. The sleigh loomed at the center of it all, a living machine of motion and rhythm. The reindeer in the distance darted and bounded, still chasing each other in lazy circles, while the red sack at the rear of the sleigh continued to be filled with gifts.

"That's Santa's sleigh?" Charli asked.

"Yes," Nog said. "Just some pre-travel preparations, that's all. The Abominables are handling most of the heavy lifting."

Charli assumed he meant the towering snowmen, still methodically loading the largest packages into the sack. The sleigh didn't groan or creak under the weight. It simply took it, as if enchanted to bear whatever the season required.

She scanned the reindeer again. The usual suspects bounded across the snow in graceful arcs, their hooves skimming the surface like dancers. But one was missing. The colossal reindeer from the island. The one with the expanse of jagged antlers and the volcanic breath. Ronin.

"Everything's on schedule," Nog continued. "It usually is, but sometimes things go a little sideways. I wouldn't say this year is completely sideways." He chuckled nervously. "Now, the worst Christmas we ever had? That would be the big storm of '83. Sleigh runners froze solid. Reindeer panic. Half the wrapping machines down..."

He began listing storms, equipment failures, delivery delays. Charli barely heard any of it. Neither did Van. Their eyes stayed fixed on the sleigh, the magic of it, the rhythm and precision, the uncanny calm.

Merry gently hushed her husband with a tap on the arm. Nog cleared his throat and went quiet. The two of them stood there, hands folded, massive feet shifting slightly in the thin dusting of snow that covered the ice.

"What day is it?" Charli asked.

"It's Christmas Eve, dear," Merry said.

It felt like they'd been gone forever. Like time had unraveled and stitched itself back together in the wrong shape. Their parents had to be looking for them by now. It was impossible to relax with that on their minds.

"What are we waiting for?" Van asked.

"They're just making final preparations," Merry replied.

"Preparations for what?"

The elves exchanged a glance. Nog rocked slightly on his heels. Then cleared his throat again.

"We can't really say much," he said. "That would be... against the rules."

"We just need to wait here," Merry added, "until they call us down."

None of that sounded reassuring. In fact, it felt a lot like sitting in a doctor's office, waiting for the nurse to come back with a syringe. You know it's coming. You don't know when. Or how much it's going to hurt.

The stars above twinkled, uncaring. The song of the elves continued behind them, but for Van and Charli, the music had become background noise.

They were waiting. And they didn't like what they were waiting for.

Van's stomach churned. Every second they stood on that ice made it worse. This was all his fault, every part of it. The hat, the island, the running. He glanced at Charli. She was chewing her lip, her wide eyes darting from one corner of the ice field to another. She felt it too. The dread twisting deeper, and there was nothing he could do to stop it.

"Look, I'm sorry for lying," he blurted. "I should've just told you where the hat was. I don't know why I didn't. I just... I panicked. I should've done the right thing."

Merry turned with a smile that was too warm, too rehearsed. "Oh, dear, it's quite all right. We understand why you did it. Not to worry. Christmas will go on. Even without the Toymaker's hat."

"The hat is still missing?"

Nog and Merry's smiles didn't move. "Everything is fine," Nog said carefully.

"Are we in trouble?" Charli asked.

"Of course not," Merry said.

"Then why can't we go home? What are we waiting for?"

"It's just taking a little time, that's all. The ice wasn't exactly designed for full-sizers like yourselves. It won't be much longer."

Van wasn't sure if that was supposed to be comforting. It wasn't. Not at all.

The music had stopped. The reindeer had stopped. Even the sack of gifts seemed to have stopped growing. The air felt still, like the entire North Pole was holding its breath.

Van didn't need to turn around to know more elves were watching them. He could feel it. He risked a glance and instantly regretted it. Too many faces. Round and pale, unmoving. Their expressions unreadable. Their stares direct.

It felt like they weren't looking at him. They were reading him. Like every mistake he'd made was laid bare, cataloged, filed away. He just wanted to go home. And yet... a part of him still didn't. Not yet.

It was a terrible feeling, wanting to escape but not knowing where to go. Not sure where he belonged.

A hole opened in the ice. Perfectly round. Silent. A dark circle at their feet, the edge so clean it didn't look real. Like the mouth of a manufactured tunnel.

Nog waddled to the edge, toes curling over the rim. He glanced back, his eyes twinkling beneath the brim of his cap. "Ever been on a water slide?"

Then he stepped forward and vanished. No scream. No sound. Just gone.

Merry stepped closer. "It's a bit of a ride for full-sizers. Just sit on the edge and drop in. Lay back, cross your arms over your chest. Let the ride take you where it's going."

A snow tunnel in the middle of the Arctic. A surprise water slide. Or ice slide. Whatever. Because why wouldn't there be one?

"I've been on water slides before," he said.

"Not like this."

They could have said no. They could have stayed right there on the ice, rooted in place while more and more elves gathered—silent and expectant, eyes wide and unblinking. They could have screamed for help, demanded answers, or refused to budge until someone explained what was happening. But that wasn't going to do anything.

Van went first and let the ride take him where it was going.

THE CHUTE WAS A SHORT, dark luge of ice that swallowed them whole. Gravity pulled them through bends and dips carved into the frozen tunnel. A thousand reflections flitted past in the ice walls—warped versions of themselves.

Voices were ahead. Dozens, maybe hundreds. All speaking at once.

They emerged into a cavernous hall to cheers and gasps and laughter. A room that wasn't tall but impossibly wide and long, its arched ceiling held up by massive pillars of crystalline ice that shimmered like chandeliers. Light came from nowhere and everywhere, bouncing off the walls in silver-blue hues.

They slid to a stop at the edge of a wide, circular platform, still on their backs. Breath puffing out clouds. Before they could sit up, two soldiers loomed above them. Tall, broad, with square jaws and painted expressions. The kind of faces that looked carved. The kind to crack nuts between oversized teeth. They reached down in perfect unison, each gripping an arm—not with force, but firm guidance—and helped them to their feet.

The hall was packed. Rows and rows of elves stood shoulder to shoulder, pressed in close, eyes locked on the newcomers. The murmurs began before Van had fully straightened.

The Nutcracker soldiers, the only full-sized beings besides Van and Charli, kept a hand on each of them—not to restrain, but to steady. The floor beneath was slick, polished to a mirror shine. A long red carpet stretched out before them, splitting the crowd in two. At the far end, Nog and Merry waited, already halfway down the aisle.

The soldiers released them once their feet touched the carpet. Elves leaned in from the sides, whispering behind their hands. A few raised tiny crystal lenses—camera-like devices that clicked and glowed to capture the moment.

Van and Charli walked. Or tried to. Even though Van stood nearly three feet taller than the tallest elf, the room felt crushing. Like being sealed inside a snow globe. There were no windows. No visible doors.

"It's impolite to stare like that," Merry called out sharply.

A few heads turned, but no one stopped watching. This wasn't curiosity. It was expectation.

Charli gripped Van's arm tightly, fingers clenched around his coat sleeve. Van felt like he had to duck, even though there was plenty of room. The air was cold enough to bite, but it was the stares and the hush of the crowd that made it hard to breathe.

Thump came from above. Dull. Rhythmic. *Thump.*

It came again. Louder this time. Something up there was moving. The ceiling shivered. Frost fell in soft crystals. A beat, like a drum. Like footsteps on the roof.

"Tell the reindeer to stop," Merry said to her husband without looking back. "The roof's too thin for games right now. They should be settling down. See if Tinsel has their final feed ready."

Nog gave a quick nod and stepped off the carpet. The moment his bare feet touched the ice, he zipped away in a blur, an impossible, gliding streak of motion that vanished into the crowd.

Meanwhile, Merry pressed forward, gently ushering Van and Charli through the thick gathering of elves. The crowd parted just enough to let them pass, though many leaned in close, eyes wide, whispers trailing in their wake.

At the far end of the chamber stood a low, frosted gate guarded by yet another Nutcracker soldier. He watched with a stillness that felt carved from stone. Beyond the gate, the space opened slightly. Two smaller tables flanked a central platform, but it was the massive desk at the front that seized Van's attention.

It stood like a frozen monument, carved entirely from crystal-clear ice, the surface etched with swirling patterns that caught and fractured the cold light. It gleamed with authority.

"What is this?"

He knew. Somewhere inside, he knew. Just like he'd known what was coming when his mom called him into the other room. It was the tone of her voice, the look on her face. This was like that. Only this time, there were elves.

And Nutcrackers.

And no way out.

"It's just a little meeting. Nothing to worry about, dear." Merry patted the back of his hand. It was meant to soothe, but it only made his nerves tighten like violin strings. "You'll be home in no time."

The Nutcracker soldier beside them gave a single nod and motioned toward the table on the left. Van and Charli moved as directed, stepping behind the frozen table. Their footsteps made soft crunches against the carpet's thin frost. Merry lingered behind a low, translucent barrier that separated the crowd from the proceedings, her expression unreadable.

To the left of them, raised bleachers curved around the space. Twelve elves sat in them, arranged like a choir. They weren't there to sing. Some leaned forward eagerly, others reclined with arms crossed, bellies round and fingers drumming. Their expressions ranged from curious to outright impatient, as if someone had interrupted their cookie breaks for this.

Van whispered out of the corner of his mouth, "This is a court."

Charli didn't look at him.

Merry's voice rose above the excitement. "Sullivan."

He flinched, hearing his legal name called out just like his mom would do. Merry smiled gently, a flicker of warmth behind the tight lines at her mouth. Then she leaned in, speaking just loud enough for him to hear:

"Just be honest. That's all you have to do."

That didn't help.

Van sat down in one of the carved chairs. It was frozen to the touch, as if his legs were being claimed by the cold. He pinched the bridge of his nose and closed his eyes. The tension in the room had mass now. It sat on his shoulders, squeezed his skull. A headache crept behind his eyes.

He'd chased a hat. He'd run through snowstorms and illusions and strange candy forests. Now he was on trial.

At the North Pole.

In front of an ice desk.

With elves.

Is there jail on the North Pole?

He didn't want to open his eyes. If he just kept them closed long enough, maybe all of this would fade away. Maybe it was just a fever dream, spun from nerves and sugar and sleep deprivation. Even the steady, rhythmic clopping overhead or the way delicate flakes of ice drifted down—none of it felt real.

The sharp clicks of cameras capturing every breath, every twitch. The low, mechanical chatter of Nutcracker soldiers as they lined up in formation, their wooden limbs creaking with precision. It all felt far away. Like it was happening to someone else. If he stayed still, if he didn't move, didn't breathe too loud, didn't open his eyes, it might stay that way.

Charli removed one of her gloves and slid her hand into his. Her fingers were stiff, but they held his with quiet strength. A reminder that she was still there. That they were in this together. Even that, though, felt like a dream.

He told himself it was enough. Her hand, her presence. As long as he didn't open his eyes, none of it had to be real. Not until someone made him.

Then the purple monkey arrived.

❄

Van opened his eyes just in time to see a small, furry figure step through a hidden doorway behind the judge's icy bench. It walked on two legs and had a tail that curled like a question mark. Its fur was violet, plush and velvety, like a stuffed animal that had come to life.

It was holding a briefcase.

The monkey waved to the jury first, then to the crowd, its stitched-on smile frozen in cheerful permanence. The elves waved back, some even clapping in delight. There were whispers of his name. If he had one, Van didn't catch it.

One of the Nutcracker soldiers hustled over with a booster chair, setting it behind the defense table. The monkey tossed the briefcase up with a practiced flip and climbed in after it, his tiny legs dangling just above the ground.

Van could only stare. A toy. A purple, plush toy. Not just any toy.

A defense attorney toy.

The monkey didn't speak. Didn't squeak or chirp or mutter a word. He moved with slow, deliberate purpose. One click at a time, he undid the brass latches on the briefcase. Inside were organized stacks of papers, photographs, and folders crammed with handwritten notes.

Van's stomach dropped. One of the pages near the top had his handwriting on it. A cold sweat began forming beneath his jacket. Where had they gotten that? Had they been watching him?

The monkey didn't acknowledge his reaction. His shiny eyes remained stationary as he flicked his head back and forth from Van to Charli. The motion was jerky, unnatural. Like a puppet being tugged on invisible strings.

Van's head throbbed, a fresh wave of nausea building behind his eyes. There was something wrong with the monkey. Not just because it didn't speak. But because it didn't blink. Didn't shift. It stared, and somehow Van felt it was expecting something.

The monkey turned, his head twitching toward the far side of the room where Merry stood. She didn't look surprised. Nog had reappeared at her side.

"They're going to need a translator," Merry said loud enough to hear. "I don't think there's time for the kids to... tune in."

What was there to translate? The purple monkey hadn't uttered a sound. No gestures, no signals, no tail flutters. Just blank, silent presence. It hadn't even blinked. But the moment Merry mentioned a translator, one of the Nutcracker soldiers snapped to attention like he'd been waiting for the cue.

Without a word, he turned and disappeared behind the judge's bench, slipping through one of the arched doorways cut into the ice.

Minutes passed. The crowd murmured, restless and curious.

Then the Nutcracker returned. He wasn't alone. Behind him waddled something that might've broken Van's brain if he hadn't already abandoned reason.

It was another toy.

This one was plush and orange. A full-sized octopus that looked like a mascot at a baseball game. It had the energy of a caffeinated party host.

Its limbs squished and squeaked as it bounced along the ice on eight tentacles. In three of those limbs, it juggled an armload of random items: a six-pack of soda cans, a candy bar half-unwrapped, and a thick stack of colorful business cards.

As it made its way toward the jury box, it handed out cards with one tentacle while tossing a soda can toward an elf with another. The elves responded with a mix of polite acceptance, blank stares, and suppressed laughter.

"Hello, hello! Nice to see you! You're looking good! Happy to be here—whoa!"

The octopus stopped abruptly at the defense table.

"We're doing kids? Ohhh, merry merry, somebody got on the Naughty List early this year!"

He turned to the far end of the table, where no chair awaited him. No problem. He curled two tentacles beneath himself and popped upright, balancing with ridiculous ease.

"The name's Ollie. I don't get up here much. North Pole, I mean. You two probably haven't seen much yet, but let me tell you something. This place is a trip. The only place where magic is real! I know, I know, it's not technically magic, but you know what I'm talkin' 'bout. Am I right?"

He shot a look toward Nog, who did not appear amused.

"Anyway," Ollie continued, "no idea how I got roped into this gig, but hey, happy to help. *Love* a crowd!"

Without breaking stride, he poured the remaining soda into what looked vaguely like a beak-shaped mouth. The entire six-pack. Then the candy bars followed, wrapper and all.

Van's mind made a feeble attempt to explain it. *Maybe... some toys are made to eat?* He couldn't believe he was actually thinking that.

"All right, let's talk turkey," Ollie said, suddenly clapping four tentacles together with surprising authority. He turned toward the purple monkey. "This is your counsel right here. His name's Monkey Brain. Monkey Brain wants you to know everything's going to be A-OK."

The purple monkey nodded slowly. Almost imperceptibly. Still silent. Still unreadable. But there was something in the posture that said *yes*.

"He wants you to know there's nothing to worry about," Ollie said, swiveling toward Van and Charli. "You're both good kids. Just a little mix-up in the peppermint pipeline, that's all. This won't take long."

Van and Charli just stared.

"So just sit back," Ollie added, "and enjoy the show."

With that, he erupted into a booming laugh that bounced off the icy pillars. Then he turned and shuffled toward the low gate, handing out more cards to anyone who would take them.

"Call me if you're ever on ToyWorld!" he sang out. "Discount legal advice and holiday parties, Ollie's got you covered!"

Van already wanted to lie down. Still trying to make sense of the surreal parade of characters and contradictions, he turned to the purple monkey.

"Why are we here?" he asked. "I'm sorry about the hat. I swear I didn't know I was taking it."

The purple monkey didn't answer. He didn't flinch. Didn't blink. Just kept that fixed, button-eyed stare, like he was either contemplating Van's words... or staring straight through him.

"Duly noted," Ollie said, nodding sharply. "Like the monkey says, that's pretty well documented. And yeah, that's about all you need to know." He adjusted a stack of files with one tentacle, then added, "He also wants to know if you've got any other questions."

"Yeah," Charli said. "When do we get home?"

Ollie looked at the monkey. The monkey didn't move. After a long pause, Ollie turned back.

"He doesn't know that." Then, without warning, he raised his voice and shouted across the courtroom. "Hey! Can we get some more winter gear over here? These two aren't cut out for this weather. Look at them! They're like two flagpoles without a flag. No offense."

A few elves giggled, muffling their laughter.

"I mean, you rub them together, you might start a fire," Ollie added with a shrug. "No offense. If they were—"

But he never finished the joke.

The temperature dropped.

It didn't just dip. It crashed. The air turned razor-sharp, each breath a cold stab. A hush rippled across the room as every head turned toward the far side of the chamber. A deep, resonant rumble vibrated underfoot. Subtle at first, then stronger. The ice beneath them seemed to hum.

Van turned slowly. His breath misted in front of him. He was sitting at a table with a purple monkey attorney and their orange octopus translator. But now entering from across the room was the oddest figure yet.

It was an elf, yes. But not like any they'd seen before. This one had no beard. No hair. No eyebrows. Not a single follicle to be found. His scalp gleamed in the pale light. But it wasn't his baldness that was stunning.

It was his skin.

Blue. Not just a soft, pastel blue. Not a sky-at-dusk blue.

Blueberry blue. Glacier blue. The deep, biting blue of winter's core.

It was a blue so vibrant and strange, it almost hurt to look at. It didn't belong. Even in this realm of magic and toys and impossible creatures.

And yet, there he was, gliding into the room like a figure skater, perfectly balanced on one foot, carving a wide circle in front of the judge's bench. One hand lifted to his ear, fingers spread in a classic "I can't hear you" pose.

But there was nothing to hear.

The room had gone utterly silent. No applause. No cheers. Just stunned, confused, waiting stillness.

The blue elf spun again, his coat flaring behind him in a dramatic swoop. With precision and flair, he completed a final turn and bowed to no one in particular.

Someone coughed.

Then he straightened and skated past the jury. Slowly. Smoothly. One finger extended like a wand, pointing at each elf with exaggerated importance. With every point, he winked. And with every wink, he said a name.

"Drizzlepop."

"Fancy Grizzle."

"Sir Marshington."

"Flufflebuns."

The names were made up, it seemed. One elf winced in confusion.

Then the blue elf coasted toward the defense table. He extended one long, elegant arm and dragged it across the surface with practiced drama, sending Monkey Brain's pens, papers, and case notes scattering across the floor like autumn leaves.

The purple monkey didn't react. Neither did Ollie.

When the elf reached Van and Charli, he stopped cold. He pointed directly at them, one finger raised like a pistol.

"You're going down," he said.

He stuck out his tongue, dark as a plum, and grinned. Not the kind of grin that screamed danger, but something sly and slippery. Mischievous, not menacing. Like a kid caught red-handed—and loving it.

"That's Jack," Ollie said, sidling closer with a wave of an empty soda can. "He's got issues."

Jack slammed his briefcase onto the table with a sound that cracked like thunder. Several elves jumped. A sticker slapped across the side read in crooked letters: *You Wish You Were Blue Too.*

He didn't open it. Instead, he slouched in his chair like a teenager bored in math class, hands laced behind his head, chair tipped so far back the legs groaned. Then he kicked his bare feet onto the table, revealing soles covered in iridescent scales that shimmered blue-green with every subtle shift. Like the belly of a fish, cold and slick.

"Ohh, this is taking forever," he groaned.

The din in the hall swelled. More elves poured in through the rear archway, trickling like ants until it became a flood. Their chatter rose into uproar, footsteps crunching across frost, laughter and debate tangling together.

Van tried saying something to Charli but couldn't hear himself, let alone her reply.

He glanced toward Jack just in time to see him dozing in place. Eyes closed. Lips fluttering with every exaggerated breath.

The cold shifted to heat, rising like someone had opened an oven door. Van unzipped his coat. Charli followed, yanking her scarf loose.

One of the Nutcracker soldiers walked calmly to the judge's bench and set a large fan beside it. When he flipped the switch, a blast of lukewarm air hummed across the room.

The crowd cheered. Applause erupted like the fan itself was the star of the show. Elves clapped with wide grins, stomping their feet, some tossing mittens into the air.

And then—*boom.*

The Nutcracker boots struck the ice in unison. The heels hit hard. Once. Twice.

It was deafening.

The sound split through the chaos like a cannon blast. Silence crashed over the room, a vacuum where breath had just been. The crowd stiffened. All eyes turned forward.

The jury rose. The spectators rose. Monkey Brain stood tall on his booster seat. Ollie balanced on his tentacles, poised like the petals of a flower. Van and Charli scrambled to their feet.

The door behind the icy judge's bench creaked open. Slow. Intentional.

From the shadows emerged a tall, wooden puppet.

He was full-sized. At least Van and Charli's height, maybe taller. His limbs moved with unnatural fluidity, like hinges that had never known rust. He climbed the judge's bench like it belonged to him.

A tall black top hat perched on his head, brushing the frost-covered ceiling. His coat fluttered as he turned, dramatic and dignified.

Then he sat.

In one sweeping motion, he threw back his robe, revealing a vivid red heart emblazoned across his chest. Not painted but carved and glowing, softly, like embers trapped in a crystal casing.

The puppet looked out at the crowd. And everyone waited.

The room was in perfect stillness, save for the soft, rhythmic snore of an elf somewhere in the gallery. The puppet judge didn't seem to notice. Or maybe he did and simply chose not to care. His carved head turned slowly, scanning the room with unblinking, painted eyes until he locked onto Jack, still lounging with his scaly feet propped on the table.

Without a word, one of the Nutcrackers marched forward, stiff as a broomstick, and tapped the table sharply.

CRACK.

The sound echoed like a nail gun on a tin roof.

Jack jolted upright, nearly flipping backward in his chair. He flailed briefly, then caught himself with a huff. A ripple of laughter passed through the crowd. Jack shot the Nutcracker a glare, but the wooden soldier stood motionless, arms at his sides, face expressionless.

"Well, merry merry, everyone," said the judge, breaking the silence.

"Merry merry," the crowd echoed in practiced unison.

"I hope everyone's feeling the Christmas spirit. I know I am." The puppet judge had a cheerful mechanical lilt, the kind of tone used in talking greeting cards, equal parts pleasant and unnerving. "I also know this is the busiest time of year, so let's get down to business."

He reached beneath the bench and pulled out a small scale of justice. Gold and perfectly polished, it swung wildly as he set it on the ice-carved desk, then slowly steadied, the trays resting in delicate equilibrium.

The judge picked up a single sheet of paper and squinted at it, holding it a little too close to his face, then too far away, then back again.

"This is the case of Jingle Jingle All the Way 459204," he said with grave importance. "We are gathered here to determine the balance of duties. Sullivan Holloway and Charlotte McNichols, how do you plead?"

The words were oddly formal for a case involving children and a hat.

Van and Charli sat stiffly, their shoulders brushing. Monkey Brain turned slowly to face them. His gaze was unreadable, but it was clear he was waiting.

Van's mind raced. It was about the hat. They'd taken it, sure. But not out of malice. It had felt like a game. Like they were supposed to take it.

"Not guilty," Van said.

A beat of silence. Then the room exploded in laughter.

Jack howled, throwing his head back. His mouth stretched wide, and even his gums were blue. He slammed a hand on the table, wiping tears from his eyes with the other, gasping for air like he'd just heard the best joke of the century.

"Children," the judge said, "this is not that kind of thing." His jaw flapped open again as he continued. "To which list should your names appear?"

Ollie leaned in from the side. "Naughty or nice."

It felt like a trick. Like answering too quickly would seal something shut forever. "N-nice," he started to say, but Charli beat him to it.

"Both," she said.

The word landed like a sleigh bell dropped in a cathedral. The courtroom went completely still. For a moment, no one moved. Then a collective gasp. It started small, a murmur of surprise through the crowd, but it grew fast. Elves clutched their coats. Several leaned forward, eyes wide.

But no one reacted quite like Jack. His hand snapped up to his mouth. His eyes went wide with shock. He stared at Charli like she'd uttered a forbidden spell.

She didn't flinch. Van looked at her in awe. Somehow, it was the right answer.

"You can't be both!" Jack barked, jumping to his feet. "They can't be both, Judge! What kind of monkey court is this?"

Monkey Brain didn't react. Neither did the judge.

"Sure, you can," Charli said. "Nobody's all one or the other."

"She's right!" Ollie hollered, flailing his tentacles. "This isn't about one list. It's about balance. Which way does it tip?"

Jack narrowed his eyes. "Who is this?"

"I'm Ollie."

"No one cares."

"The kids don't have the... you know." Ollie tapped his head. "They can't connect."

"Whoa-whoa." Jack raised both hands, fingers splayed. "You're sayin' these two naughty warmbloods—"

"Objection, your honor!" Ollie shouted, shooting up on two tentacles.

"Allegedly naughty warmbloods," Jack corrected with an exaggerated eye-roll. "You're sayin' they can't even hear their own attorney?"

Monkey Brain, for his part, didn't move. Ollie sighed.

"It's not a hearing problem, Jack. It's a tuning problem. They aren't wired for it. You know this. And warmblood is completely uncalled for. If you think we're just going to—"

"Oh, I know what it needs," Jack interrupted. "Takes a certain kind of resonance, right? Emotional syncing, holiday frequency, blah-blah-blah. And let me guess—these two just haven't had enough eggnog and life-changing revelations to sync up yet?"

"That's... not an entirely unfair description," Ollie muttered.

"So we're wasting time in a courtroom with two clueless meat puppets who can't even hear the monkey they hired to save their hides?" Jack asked the judge, spreading his arms. "How's that for due process?"

The puppet judge tilted his head. "Counsel," he said, "you will refer to the children as children. Not meat puppets."

"Warmbloods, then," Jack offered.

"Children," the judge said.

Jack collapsed back into his chair. "Fine. Children. Allegedly."

Van looked to Ollie. "So how do we connect to Monkey Brain? What do we have to do?"

"That's... a little complicated," Ollie said.

Jack cackled. "Understatement of the century."

The judge reached for his gavel and banged it once.

Squeak.

Jack kept talking. The judge banged it again.

SQUEAK-SQUEAK-SQUEAK.

The gavel's shrill, rubber-duck squeal filled the chamber until Jack finally clenched his jaw and backed off. The crowd snickered.

Once silence returned, the judge cleared his throat. "I'm aware this is about balance, counsel," he said, pointing to the scales, which now tipped ever so slightly. "But the children must state which side they fall on. Naughty... or nice?"

"Nice, your honor," Charli said.

"Of course you'd say that," Jack snarled. "It's obvious they're naughty. And I'm not talking about when they were toddlers and didn't know better. I'm talking this year. I'm talking now. And I'm going to prove it. Easily. Without even trying." He slammed his fist on the table. "This is going to be the easiest thing I've ever done."

"Hear, hear!" someone in the crowd shouted.

The judge squeaked the gavel again. When order returned, he said, "Defense, you may call your first witness."

Monkey Brain tilted his head at Van and Charli. The moment stretched awkwardly, a long silence filled only by the faint hum of the fan.

"Do either of you have someone who can say something nice?" Ollie said.

"What?" Van said. "We don't even know where we are. Nobody here knows us."

"Soooo... no?"

"No, Ollie. We don't," Charli said. "Unless you want to go up there."

"I just met you." Ollie threw his limbs in the air. "What would I say? 'They seem chill'?"

"Better than nothing," she said.

Ollie paused, processing. Then raised a tentacle. "That's a big N-O, your honor. They have no one who can say anything nice about them."

A collective gasp swept through the courtroom. Jack burst out laughing.

"So easy," he cackled.

"No!" Charli shouted. "That's not what we mean! We have friends. We have family. They're just not here. You have to know that, right? We don't live here!"

"You've got those... those lookie things," Van added. "The ones that record stuff. Use them. You can see everything we've done. Everything we've said. We're not perfect, but we're not—"

"Naughty," Charli finished.

Ollie's eyebrows (which may have been drawn on) arched thoughtfully. The judge stroked his chin with a clunky wooden hand. Even Monkey Brain's head tilted, the gears inside faintly whirring.

And the scales... shifted. Just a hair toward nice.

He wasn't sure how that would help.

The jury didn't need a reminder that he was the one who'd woken up with the Toymaker's hat stuffed in his pocket. The same hat he'd lied about. The same lie that kicked all this off. Someone who actually knew them, someone from their world should've been the one to speak on their behalf. But no one was here.

The gavel squeaked again.

"The court recognizes that witnesses for the defense are not present," the puppet judge declared, "but that they exist. Duly noted."

"So easy," Jack muttered, again.

"Wait! Your honor, can we approach the bench?" Ollie called out.

"I guess," the judge replied with a shrug. "Or you could just say it."

Monkey Brain pointed at the judge. It wasn't much of a movement, just a simple gesture, but somehow the judge seemed to get it. He nodded once in understanding.

"Objection!" Jack was on his feet immediately. "Objection to whatever that was!"

"He's telling them we have some evidence," Ollie muttered. "Trust me. You're going to be all right."

A pair of Nutcracker soldiers wheeled something into the courtroom. A boxy, ancient-looking television. The kind with wood paneling and dials the size of doorknobs. Its gray screen stared blankly ahead.

"What is that?" Jack shrieked. "That's not evidence. Fake news! That's—you're making a mockery of this monkey court!"

"Overruled," said the judge without looking up.

"What? You can't overrule me! This whole court is overruled!"

Laughter erupted from all corners. Some elves stood and shouted back at Jack. Others wheezed with laughter, doubling over and snapping pictures with candy-cane-colored cameras. It felt more like the end of a talent show gone off the rails.

And yet, through the laughter and chaos, Van noticed something strange. Merry and Nog weren't laughing. They weren't even smiling. Their faces were stone-still, eyes locked on the television with cold intensity.

The judge raised a remote the size of a brick with buttons and clicked it several times.

The TV hissed with static. Then the screen flickered to life.

A ghostly gray glow spilled over the courtroom as the footage began to play.

THE SCREEN CRACKLED, lines of static zigzagging across the image. The theme song bounced along, unnaturally cheerful, like something from an ancient sitcom lost in time.

The Nice Life appeared in bold, sparkling letters across the screen. The font was rounded and friendly, glittering like tinsel. The title lingered a beat before fading into a sweeping shot of a grand suburban house with trimmed hedges and a swing set in the yard. The music softened into something whimsical, like chimes drifting through a candy store.

"If you want to see the nice things Sullivan and Charlotte have done," the narrator said, in an old-timey, tinny voice echoing from a laundry vent, "you don't have to look far! Take, for example, Charlotte. She can be found paying for her friends' lunches, especially those who are hungry and don't have enough money."

A grainy video played: Charli at a school cafeteria checkout, casually tapping her card while three girls in cheer uniforms stood behind her, laughing and smiling. She paid and kept moving, brushing hair out of her eyes like it was no big deal.

"Give me a break," Jack muttered.

"She's also very popular, very pretty, and she studies every night to get very good grades."

The screen transitioned to Charli at her desk. A warm desk lamp glowed over a jungle of papers and highlighters. Her face was tired but focused, her pencil moving steadily over a worksheet. In the background, a digital clock blinked 12:17 AM.

"Pretty? That's not the same thing as nice." He turned toward the jury box. "You know that, right? Don't fall for the—"

"Just listen to what her chemistry teacher said about her," the narrator cut in.

Miss Barney, framed by beakers and a wall of faded periodic tables, appeared on-screen.

"Charlotte is just like a beam of sunshine that walks into the classroom," she said, smiling behind thick glasses. "I've been teaching for almost 30 years, and I've never had a student quite like her. Always the first one in, always the last one to leave. Her homework is always done. She could possibly be the best student I've ever had."

"Objection!" Jack shouted, springing to his feet. "Objection! Objection!"

"Sit down," the judge said, casually squeaking the gavel.

"But—!"

Squeak.

The narrator pressed on. "And not far away, Sullivan was doing nice things in his neighborhood."

The footage switched to Van, outside a grocery store on a cloudy morning. A crushed soda can bounced across the lot. He picked it up without hesitation and dropped it into the nearest bin.

"He picks up litter," the narrator said. "Even when no one is watching."

More clips followed: Van helping a neighbor carry groceries to their porch; standing outside a convenience store, giving a dollar to a kid short on change.

"He walks his dog every morning for fifteen minutes," the narrator added.

"OMG!" Jack stood again. "These are tiny things! That's not nice, that's just basic human behavior!"

The judge raised the gavel but only brought it halfway down. Jack cringed.

"Defense may continue," the judge said. "Good stuff."

The TV flickered again. More footage loaded. More quiet acts. More quiet truths. Van's shoulders eased. Maybe they didn't need a witness after all.

The screen held on a soft, quiet moment of Van kneeling down to attach the leash to Lenny's collar. The dog wagged his tail, licking Van's cheek once before the two set off down a sunlit sidewalk. Their steps were unhurried and easy, underscored by the gentle rhythm of wholesome, plucky music.

"It's a dog," Jack grunted. "He walks him because he has to."

The camera cut to another scene: Van at a checkout counter in a small grocery store. He handed over a twenty-dollar bill. The cashier, clearly distracted, gave him back a fat wad of change. Van paused, stared at it, then without hesitation, slid a few bills back across the counter.

"Here he is, giving money back to a cashier when he was given the wrong change," the narrator said. "And we're not talking pennies. Sullivan gave back almost forty dollars."

Gasps rippled through the jury. Some elves nodded in approval. One dabbed at their eyes with a mitten. Another blew their nose into a festive handkerchief.

Jack's ears turned a deeper shade of blue. Even he had to admit forty bucks was no joke.

"I would've gotten in big trouble," said Chad, the cashier. Chad looked like the kind of teenager who stocked shelves during the week and ran the register on weekends. He had acne, a hoodie, and wide eyes.

"I mean, I'll be honest," Chad said, "I don't know if I would've given back that much money. It was a lot. I would've been in so much trouble. Van's like... he's like a superhero, honestly."

Van stared at the screen, stunned. He hadn't even remembered that moment. But it had happened. The soda can, the dog walks were small things. But the money? That had been a choice. A big one.

Charli squeezed his hand.

"Come oooon!" Jack shouted, throwing his arms up so hard his chair toppled backward. "Are you kidding me with that? That was the dumbest thing I've ever seen! It's so fake news. You all see that, right? The fakest!" He spun toward the jury. "You really think people are gonna interview someone over giving back money? Why would he give back that much money? The kid gave it to him! It was his at that point! That's not nice. It's dumb."

Monkey Brain made a slow, deliberate gesture with two fingers, then a palm down. Ollie nodded, folding his tentacles like he was finishing a prayer.

"We rest our case, Your Honor."

"Rest your face," Jack sneered, yanking his chair upright.

"Order! Order!" the puppet judge bellowed, squeaking his gavel. Glaring at Jack.

"Your Honor, if I may? These are obviously two really good kids," Ollie said, sweeping a tentacle toward Van and Charli. "Have they made mistakes? What kid hasn't? That's how warmbloods learn. Am I right?"

"Counselor," the puppet judge warned. "Language."

"My apologies," Ollie said, bowing slightly toward Van and Charli. "These humans. These kids. They learn from their mistakes. That's how they grow. Take a good look at them. I've only known them for a minute, but I've watched. I've listened and learned. And I can tell they're not perfect. But they are good. To the core, your honor."

Van didn't speak. Charli didn't move.

The balance on the scale shifted. And this time, it tipped toward nice.

Ollie delivered his closing words with the poise of a showman and the precision of a seasoned lawyer, his tentacles curling like punctuation marks on every heartfelt phrase. The courtroom responded with a polite scattering of applause. A few elves even stomped their boots in appreciation. Ollie gave a small bow then turned back toward the judge, tentacles folded behind his back.

Jack stuck a finger in his mouth and gagged.

The scale of justice, perched atop the judge's icy bench, had tipped dramatically toward Van and Charli's side. It was a landslide.

"Is it my turn?" Jack reached into his briefcase. "Well, hey—look what I've got."

He pulled out a sleek, glossy blue remote. It shimmered like tinsel and looked more like a gaming controller than a courtroom tool. Jack stroked one long fingernail across the glowing buttons. His dark tongue flicked over his lips, that shark-like grin growing wider.

Monkey Brain jumped up and down on the defense table.

"This evidence wasn't shared with us!" Ollie shouted.

"I don't have to share anything with you!" Jack barked. "I don't even know you." He placed one dramatic hand over his heart and turned to the judge. "My apologies, Your Honor. It seems opposing counsel doesn't know what they're doing. If I may?"

"Go on."

"Thank you, Your Excellency," Jack said with an exaggerated bow.

He raised the remote and clicked. The television sputtered with static again. But this time, the cheerful glow was gone. The music warped, slowed, and shifted into something darker. The narrator's voice returned. It was deeper with a sarcastic edge. As if a sneer were a person.

"If you think these two are angels, then you're dumber than you look."

The crowd murmured.

"Let's start with Sullivan, the boy who stole a toy from his cousin. A toy he liked. A toy he shoved in his pocket and took home on purpose. A toy that made his cousin cry. A toy Sullivan hid from his parents."

The image appeared: a grainy, grainy video clip of a younger Van, no more than seven, crouched beside his cousin Bobby's toy race-track. He reached out, paused, then grabbed a shiny red and silver car. He glanced over his shoulder. Then he slipped it into his hoodie pocket.

The video paused on the moment he turned away. Gasps rippled through the crowd. A few elves exchanged horrified looks. The jury buzzed with quiet murmurs. Even a Nutcracker soldier's jaw dropped.

Van remembered it all. The weight of the car. The way it sparkled. How badly he'd wanted it. And the sick twist in his gut later, when Bobby cried and no one knew why.

"Uh, Your Honor?" Ollie piped up. "I thought we weren't doing things from when they were little."

"Shh. There's more," Jack whispered.

"How about when he washes the dishes?" the narrator continued. "A daily chore. But when his mom and dad aren't watching, he just rinses them. No soap. No scrubbing. Just a splash of water and a lie."

The screen showed Van in the kitchen, glancing over his shoulder, then running a plate under the tap for two seconds before stacking it with the rest.

The narrator added, "Even when asked if the dishes were washed, our little angel says, 'Sure are.'"

Van didn't need the video to remember that one. It had been last week. The lie had slipped out so easily, like it was made of butter. He'd been tired. He just didn't feel like doing the dishes. And the shame in his chest was squirming.

The crowd reacted again, a few more gasps and low murmurs of disapproval. A grunt or two came from the jury.

Jack aimed the remote like he was about to pause it. "Psych."

"And what about the time he kicked the soccer ball through a window?" the narrator went on. "Oh yeah. He kicked it as hard as he could, right through Mrs. Colax's bedroom window."

A pause, just long enough for the image to sharpen into the fuzzy memory of a soccer ball sailing in slow motion through glass.

The screen flickered again. A new scene loaded.

Mrs. Colax sat in a floral recliner, framed by lace curtains and old family photographs. Her living room was cozy and warm, the glow of a muted television flickering in the background. Her hands were folded in her lap.

"I was in the front room, watching my program," she said. "I heard a big crash. Thought maybe someone had dropped something heavy outside. But I didn't go to look. Not right away. It wasn't until I was doing laundry and walked into my bedroom that I saw the glass. All over my bed. Tiny shards... everywhere. I didn't sleep in it for weeks. Not because I couldn't replace the mattress, but because I just couldn't get the feeling out of my head."

She paused, eyes distant.

"I kept thinking... who would do such a thing? Who would do something like that... and not say anything?"

The screen held on her face. Not angry. Just... tired. Wounded. The kind of quiet hurt that had nothing to do with broken glass.

The courtroom was utterly silent. No whispers. No reactions. Just the crackle of the old TV, the flicker of frost reflecting off its screen.

Van remembered the wild kick. The sickening crash. The sprint home with his lungs burning and the panic rising. He hadn't just felt guilty. He'd been haunted. He didn't eat. Didn't talk. He told his parents he was sick and stayed home, curled up in bed like he could hide from the truth.

For two weeks, he avoided eye contact with anyone. And for two years, he kept the memory buried. The longer he waited to confess, the heavier it became. Until it wasn't just guilt, it was something worse.

Across the room, some elves leaned toward one another, whispering quietly. A few shook their heads. Others just stared.

The jury looked restless now, elbows shifting on chair arms, fingers steepled beneath twitching chins. The softness that had bloomed during Ollie's speech was retreating under the cold light of consequence.

The scale of justice teetered. It rocked slowly left, then right. Then left again.

Its delicate balance began to sway, pendulum-like, caught in the storm of two truths of kindness and mistakes, generosity and guilt. The room held its breath. The verdict hadn't been spoken.

"Angel number two, come on down!" Jack bellowed, spreading his arms. His wicked blueberry grin practically glowed. "Let's see what she's been hiding. How about a little cheating, for starters?"

He wagged a long, ink-blue finger at the audience, drawing out the pause, wallowing in the tension.

"Ohh yeah, Little Miss Goody Goody paid someone to do her homework. And not just once."

There was Charli, smiling wide as she handed her parents a

paper with a bold red A+ scribbled across the top. Her mom hugged her. Her dad clapped her on the back. Their faces glowing with pride.

At the defense table, Charli's eyes dropped to the floor. Her face, suddenly pale, gave nothing away.

"But wait, there's more! Tell 'em what she won, Johnny!" Jack cupped his hand to his ear. "She ran into a car!"

The footage rolled. Charli, behind the wheel of her parents' sedan. Grocery store parking lot. Blinker on. Bam! The front bumper nudged into the side of a brand-new, candy-red pickup truck. A metallic scrape followed. Her eyes widened.

She panicked. No getting out. No note. She backed up and pulled away.

And the scene continued with the truck's owner outside the store. He was rugged, sunburned, and still in work boots, his shirt streaked with drywall dust. A sleepy toddler perched on his hip, clinging to his collar with a juice-stained hand.

"I just bought this truck a month ago," he said, gently bouncing the girl. "I'm barely startin' payments on it. Never had a new ride before. Never in my life. I was inside, what, five minutes? And I come out to this?"

He gestured to the dent, big enough to notice, deep enough to hurt.

"They didn't leave a note. Least they could do."

The courtroom shifted. The elves in the jury winced, some lowering their eyes. A couple shook their heads. Groans of disappointment rolled like thunder through the cavern.

For a moment, Van and Charli didn't notice the ice walls. Or the oversized Nutcracker guards. Or the purple monkey silently bouncing on his toes.

They weren't in some magical courtroom anymore. They were just two kids caught in the gravity of their own choices.

One of the Nutcracker soldiers wheeled the TV away. The squeaky wheel echoed through the chamber like a final gavel strike.

The Scales of Justice above the judge's bench trembled. They rocked wildly, tilting this way and that, unbalanced. Uncertain. The needle looked like it was leaning toward nice. Barely.

Ollie whispered out of the corner of his mouth. "I think we got it."

But Jack wasn't done.

"The hat! I can't believe I almost forgot the hat!"

He broke into a chaotic tap dance in front of his table, feet clattering across the ice, arms pumping like a deranged wind-up toy. He twirled in a full circle and pointed skyward.

"The hat, the hat, the very important hat!" he sang. "Everybody remembers the hat, right? Remember what happened to it? Remember how everyone went looking for it? And remember how Christmas has been practically ruined?"

He stomped his foot. A sharp CRACK! rang through the chamber like a whip across a lake. And then his finger cut the air like a dagger, aimed directly on Van.

"He stoooooooole it."

Gasps exploded from the jury. The elves jumped to their feet, shouting over one another. The room roared like a furnace on full blast.

"Is that true?"

"That's the kid?"

"How could he—?"

"Ruined everything!"

Ollie waved his tentacles. "It wasn't his fault! He didn't even know he was stealing it!"

The puppet judge slammed the gavel but the squeaky little hammer barely made a dent in the noise.

And yet the Scales of Justice didn't budge. Not an inch.

It had already tallied that mistake. Already weighed it. Maybe it even understood it. Because Van hadn't meant to steal the hat. It had found its way to him.

But Jack saw it too. Saw that delicate stillness. That minuscule tilt.

He was losing. By the width of a snowflake.

"I call my one and only witness!" Jack bellowed.

Gasps again. More stomping. And that sharp and blue finger swung back around. And landed on Van.

Another eruption from the crowd. The entire cavern seemed to tremble. Tiny shards of frost dusted the courtroom like powdered sugar, shaken loose from the ceiling.

"ORDER! ORDER!" the puppet judge bellowed, whacking the gavel like a child slapping a toy drum.

Van turned, scanning the blur of motion and shouting. That's when he saw Merry. She wasn't yelling. She wasn't moving. She was watching him. Mouth forming silent words.

He leaned closer. Stooped down. Her breath was cool, peppermint sweet.

"Be honest, dear," she whispered, almost too quiet to hear.

Be honest? He was telling the truth. What did she mean by that?

One of the Nutcrackers stepped forward, resting a heavy wooden hand on Van's shoulder. Not harsh, but firm. He was guided to a small chair near the puppet judge's bench, facing the crowd, facing the scales, facing everything.

Ollie was by his side in a heartbeat. "Don't answer a single question. Not one. You hear me? Don't give him anything to twist."

Van wasn't sure that was an option.

Jack took center stage like a host stepping into his spotlight. He raised his hands slowly, calling for quiet. The noise tapered. The jury settled. Even the Nutcracker soldiers at the doors stood straighter.

Jack's gaze flicked to the scales, then to Van. "Well, well, well. Here we are again."

"What?" Van said.

"Was I talking to you?"

Jack started pacing, pressed his fingers together, thoughtful. Dramatic.

"You're a little liar," he said. "Would that be fair to say?"

The courtroom held its breath. Even the scales shivered.

"Sometimes," Van said.

"Good. Good. I, um, didn't expect you to answer that, but good." Jack began to circle like a wolf in the snow. "Let's tell a little story then, shall we? Just to make sure we've got our facts straight."

He slid with precision, weaving a net of words.

"Once upon a time, there was a young man. He was small. Not in body, but in presence. So small, so insignificant, he barely existed. In a room full of people, he was alone. Sound familiar?"

Van's fingers dug into his knees.

"And then there's her," Jack said, eyes flashing toward Charli. "He watches you. Did you know that? Oh yeah. He sits behind her in class and stares at the back of her head. Sometimes he counts the hairs. He's obsessed!"

A few gasps fluttered from the crowd.

"She's so pretty. And he's so not. And she's so popular. And he's just soooo..." Jack let it hang. Then: "Not."

Jack turned, scanning the jury box. Then bent closer to Van.

"How am I doing so far?"

The room had gone silent, the kind of silence that stands on your chest. Even the Scales of Justice gave a quiet creak, like they were straining under the weight.

Van's hands were clenched so tightly his knuckles had gone white. Then, slowly, he gave a small nod.

A sharp gasp from the jury. A few heads turned toward Charli.

"Righteo!" Jack clapped his hands together. "And then he went to her house for a party. Ladies and gentlemen, how do you think that went? Picture it, folks. The girl of his dreams, sitting on the floor, in the glow of tree lights. And get this. She remembered him. She actually knew his name! Oooooo-ooo-ooo, how about that? And what do you think he did?"

Jack wheeled back toward Van.

"He leaned against the wall. Stood there like a statue, watching. He didn't have the stones to look her in the eye. To say her name. To even utter a merry, merry."

A soft murmur pulsed through the room. The Scales of Justice began to sway back and forth.

"Until the glasses came out," Jack said, almost purring now. "That was something, wasn't it? Because you know how to play games, don't you? You know. And when you showed her how, she looked at you, didn't she?"

Jack leaned closer.

"I'm asking you, Sullivan. She saw you, didn't she?"

Van's shoulders sagged. "Yeah."

He could feel it again, the lift of her smile, the way her eyes actually saw him. Not through him. Not past him. Him.

"He was going to impress her, yes he was! For the first time in his life, he was going to be seen. He was going to be popular. And you were, weren't you? You were almost there."

Van didn't answer. Jack didn't care.

"You could've gone home that night and it would've been the best night of your entire life. But nooo. You had to go and steal the hat, didn't you?"

"I didn't know," Van said. "I didn't know it was stealing."

"Ohhh, you didn't know? Then tell me this." He stopped center stage and made exaggerated air quotes. "Why did you lie about where you hid it, huh? Why lie if you 'didn't know'?"

All eyes were on him. And all Van could feel was the truth trying to claw its way up.

"I... I don't know."

Jack spun toward the jury. "Did you hear that? He lied about the hat! He liiiiiiied!"

He jabbed a finger toward Van, then the jury, demanding judgment.

"Admit it to them. Say it. Look them in the eyes and admit it!"

Van's heart pounded, but he looked up. The twelve elves on the jury watched him, their faces a mosaic of sternness, sympathy, and suspicion. He made himself meet their gaze.

"I did lie," he said. "I don't know why. Maybe... maybe I just didn't want this to end. Whatever this is. I've never felt like this before. And

I guess I just wanted it to last a little longer." He let out a shaky breath, shaking his head. "I wasn't trying to hurt anyone. And to be honest? I didn't even think this was real."

A soft murmur rippled through the crowd. Not judgment, but the sound of hearts cracking open. The jury of elves shifted in their seats, their cold professionalism melting just slightly. One elf blinked a little too fast. Another nodded, almost imperceptibly.

Jack's face flushed an unnatural shade of purple. His jaw tensed, lips pressed into a line. He turned toward the Scales of Justice. They moved.

Against him.

Not fast. Not dramatic. But enough.

Van had been honest. Not perfect. Not blameless. But honest. And that counted for more than Jack had planned for.

"You don't believe in Santa, isn't that right?" Jack barked.

Whatever compassion had begun to bloom was immediately stepped on. The elves didn't breathe. The room didn't echo. Every elf leaned forward. Some rose to their feet. Others pressed recording devices to their lips. The moment felt cosmic.

Van had seen so many strange things. Unexplainable things that walked and talked. But he had not seen Santa Claus.

"No," he said. "I don't."

A shockwave pulsed through the cavern, spiderwebbing cracks across the base of the puppet judge's bench. Somewhere high above, a chandelier of ice trembled.

But the Scales didn't flinch. They remained firmly in Van's favor. Because not believing in Santa didn't make him naughty.

"All right," the puppet judge said, rising. "I think we've heard enough."

"Wait! Wait, wait, wait!"

Jack lunged, hands outstretched, trying to snatch the gavel. The judge yanked it away with a wooden snap.

"Really, Jack?" the judge said flatly. "Will you just get on with it? It's Christmas!"

"I'm almost there." His eyes bulged. "Give it a second."

Jack tugged at his coat lapels, pacing in tight circles. His breath steamed. Beads of frost-sweat dotted his bald blue head. He wiped his face, and they scattered like shattered glass across the floor.

He turned. And when he stepped in front of Van again, he wasn't unraveling anymore. He was Jack again. Smiling. Dangerous. And very, very calm.

"You like her, don't you?"

"Your honor, come on already!" Ollie cried. Monkey Brain shook his fists in protest, nearly tumbling from his booster chair. "Are we starting over?"

"Just answer the question," Jack said. "Simple yes or no. Likey? No likey?"

He wagged his finger like a metronome. The room leaned in— judge, jury, even the guards. Every elf holding their breath.

Van felt it. The pressure. Like the whole world had narrowed to this moment.

He nodded.

"Tell us something we don't know. The way you stare at her in class? I mean, get a room. And let's not forget how you follow her on social media, too. Don't deny it. That's not a question. We know you do." Jack let it hang there. The slow drip of embarrassment. "It's pretty clear you're obsessed. I mean... it's embarrassing. Wouldn't you say?"

Van swallowed. His throat felt sandpaper dry. He nodded once.

"I know. Ooooh, I know."

Jack turned and strutted toward his table like a man who thought he'd won. It seemed like he was about to rest his case.

"Oh. One more thing."

He reached into his briefcase, the sound of the snap echoed unnaturally loud in the frozen hush. Slowly, dramatically, he pulled something out and held it between two fingers. He lifted it high so the light caught its rough, copper-brown surface.

"You know what this is?" he said, showing it to the jury. "It's a nail, ladies and gentlemen. A simple little thing. Nothing special. His step-father, good ol' Petey keeps them in a jar in the garage. Rusty ten-penny nails. Weird, right? That they use the word penny to measure nails? You know why they do that?"

"Objection!" Ollie shouted. "Is this ever going to end?"

Van barely heard him. His eyes were fixed on the nail.

Heat rose in his chest like a fever, even in the frigid air. His cheeks burned. His heart thudded.

He knew what was coming.

Jack turned toward Charli. "Did he tell you? Oh, what the heck. Bring the TV back in. Maybe we've got ourselves a little after school special to help explain."

"I did it!" Van couldn't take it. The words burst from his mouth. "I did it!"

Nobody moved. Nobody gasped. They didn't understand. Not yet. Not even Charli.

Van's stomach flipped. He would've told the whole story, right then, spilled everything. But it was too late. The Nutcracker had wheeled the TV back in. The screen flickered to life.

A grocery store parking lot. Late afternoon light. Still and quiet.

There he was. Him. Van. Looking around. Holding the nail.

Pretending to tie a shoe that didn't need tying, then slipping the sharp, rusty point into the tread of a truck tire.

The video froze on his face. Mid-act. Not just guilty. Deliberate.

The courtroom remained dead quiet. Not a sound.

The Scales of Justice stopped swaying. They had found their still point. It wasn't where they were before.

For one, suspended second, the courtroom was ice. Then came the gasps. Little hands flew to little mouths. Elves stared in horror. Jaws dropped. Tiny breaths caught in throats. And they didn't even know the full story.

Charli did.

Van couldn't bring himself to look at her. Not now. Maybe not ever again.

"Ladies and gentlemen of the jury," Jack boomed, "and to the esteemed crowd packed in here today. That truck belonged to Charlotte's boyfriend!"

He pointed, slow and theatrical.

"Her boyfriend is not this boy right here. Sullivan Holloway, deliberately and with full knowledge of what a nail will do to a tire, no matter how fat and knobby it is, put that nail against it."

Every word hit like a hammer.

"Sullivan put a nail in the tire. You're getting the picture, right?"

He let it linger. The silence inside Van roared louder than the crowd.

"That boy, Charlotte's boyfriend, he used his own money to fix that tire. Because Van was jealous. And that, ladies and gentlemen of the jury..." Jack dropped to a whisper. "That's what we call... naughty."

He took one elegant step back. Lifted an invisible basketball. Shot. Held his hand in the air like the arc was perfect. Then pumped his fist, raising one finger in victory.

The Scales of Justice tipped. All the way.

The courtroom erupted. Cheers, stomps, claps, voices overlapping in chaos. Some elves celebrated. Some simply shouted. The sound of feet on frost made the whole cavern quake.

And in the center of it all, Van stood still. "I'm sorry!" he cried out. "I didn't mean to—"

But the words vanished. Swallowed by noise. Drowned.

Charli wasn't looking at him anymore.

"He did it! He did it, he did it, he did it!" Jack howled, arms lifted like he'd just won the North Pole Cup. "That's what we're here for, folks! Am I right? I mean, come on, am I right?!"

"It was a crime of passion!" Ollie the octopus shouted from the defense table, raising all eight tentacles. "I've done worse! Way worse! I hit cars all the time! And sometimes on purpose! Not to any of you, of course, but, you know—sometimes I just hit a car. It's what I do."

"You're on trial next, you eight-legged freak!" Jack roared.

"GOOD! I don't care!" Ollie shouted back. "I'm naughty all the way!"

Laughter broke out. Shouting. Pounding. Cameras flashing. The court crumbled into a storm of confusion. The line between trial and spectacle vanished. And beneath it all, like a flame lost in the wind, the Christmas spirit flickered.

No one could hear it anymore. Not over the noise.

Van didn't want to be there. He didn't want to be anywhere. He didn't want Charli to look at him. Disbelief was carved into her face. Her lips were parted like she might speak, but the words never came.

How could he explain what he'd done when he didn't even understand it? It hadn't been planned. Not like a villain twisting a mustache. It wasn't evil. Just... wrong.

His stomach twisted with something rotten and unmovable. Guilt? Shame? Some blend of both. It didn't matter. It hurt.

It was out now. No more hiding. At least... not from her.

She looked so confused. So betrayed. And Van didn't want to be the reason for that. He didn't want this to be the part she remembered.

So he took a step. Just one.

His voice was gone, stolen by everything that had come before. But in his heart, just one thing pulsed like a desperate bell.

I'm sorry.

Not because it would fix anything. But because it was all he had left.

JACK HURLED his briefcase at Ollie. It spun through the air and struck the table with a loud crack. The latch snapped open, spewing papers in every direction like a startled flock of birds.

Ollie ducked, then retaliated with a flurry of empty soda cans. They clanked off Jack's shoulders and bounced across the icy courtroom floor.

Then, with a roar that came from somewhere deep and furious, Ollie flipped the table.

Elves sprang from the jury box in high-pitched alarm. The puppet judge launched his tiny gavel into the brawl, the little mallet spinning like a toy helicopter. Snowballs flew from unseen corners.

Nutcrackers clattered into motion, their heavy wooden limbs struggling to keep pace. They tried to restrain the elves, but the court barricade collapsed under their giant feet. The elves surged forward, faces wild, eyes bright with confusion and mischief. They stormed the judge's bench, then hesitated.

No one gave a command. No one knew why they had charged.

So they danced.

First one, then another, then all of them. They jumped up and down, linked arms, and spun in dizzying circles. Their voices collided in song, each one singing something different. It was a jumbled, clashing mess of carols and chants, like someone turning the dial on a dozen old radios.

And yet, the chaos became a kind of shield. A swirling, bouncing, foot-stomping barrier that kept Jack and Ollie from tearing each other apart.

Somewhere in the noise, the purple monkey slipped away. His work was finished. He didn't know what Van had done to Charli's boyfriend's truck. Maybe no one did.

It didn't matter. Van was guilty. *Naughty.*

Van sank into the witness chair. Around him, the madness raged like a snowstorm, but inside him it was worse.

The ceiling above was dusted with what looked like snow. No, not snow. Ice. Sharp as splinters. They drifted down like glass dust in a broken world. From somewhere above came the sound of hooves.

Then came the crack.

It started small. A hairline fracture that crept across the ceiling. It zigzagged, then curved, then split again. By the time it reached the far wall, it had become a web. And it was moving.

It slithered downward, creeping between icicles and stone, disappearing beneath the blur of stomping feet.

Van cupped his hands around his mouth and shouted. No one heard. His voice was another instrument in the orchestra of chaos. He screamed Charli's name.

He turned in a slow, frantic circle, searching. Where she had been was now only a mess of overturned chairs and broken candy-cane railing.

He shoved into the dancing elves, slipping between whirling arms and clapping hands. They laughed as they spun, blind to his struggle. Their feet slapped the floor. Their songs clashed and overlapped, becoming one long, discordant chant.

Van stumbled past a fallen nutcracker, clambered over a collapsed bench, and finally reached the overturned table.

Charli was huddled low, knees tucked to her chest, hands clasped in her lap. Her head hung, her hair hiding her face. Van dropped to his knees beside her.

"Hey," he said. Quietly. Gently. But everything in him was screaming.

She didn't look up. He wasn't even sure if she had heard him. Even if she had, what could he possibly say that wouldn't make it worse? He wanted to tell her he was sorry.

Sorry for the mess. Sorry for the stress.

If he hadn't helped her put the glasses on, if he had just walked away that night at the café, none of this would have happened. But what good would it do now, to say that? What good would it do to apologize when the world was cracking open and a dozen elves were singing twelve different songs at once? He also wanted to tell her something else.

This was the best Christmas ever.

That even with all the chaos, the danger, the embarrassment, the guilt... somehow, it still meant something. He felt both naughty and nice. And it was strange, holding those two feelings in the same heart.

Without thinking, he placed his hand gently on her arm. It wasn't calculated. It wasn't brave. It just happened.

Her hair shifted slightly, and her eyes met his.

She wasn't mad. Not scared. She looked... concerned.

But not in that distant, polite way people look at someone when they're sad and don't know what else to do. This was the kind of concern that came from someone who had been there. The kind that said, *I know what this feels like.*

The kind that said, *Me too.*

She looked like someone whose heart had cracked open too many times, and she was still trying to hold the pieces together. Someone who knew what it was like to sit in the back row, not because it was her favorite, but because it was safe.

Someone who knew what it was like to want friends. Someone who hoped, just once, that the person they really liked would look over and see them. Really see them.

Maybe she saw all of that in him now. Or maybe Van was imagining it.

He sat down beside her, crossed his legs, and leaned his back against the overturned table.

They didn't speak. They didn't know what was supposed to happen next. And strangely, that was okay.

The courtroom still buzzed like a snow globe with a loose screw. Elves kept spinning. Stomping. Singing. The nutcrackers had long since abandoned order. No one was rushing over to drag them off to a naughty jail. No one was scribbling their names in red ink. No one even seemed to notice them anymore.

Charli hadn't done anything to go to naughty jail. She wasn't the one who flattened Bobby's tire. She hadn't crouched behind the wheel, holding a nail like it was some kind of vengeance wand.

What was the worst thing Charli had ever done? Cheated on homework? Maybe. Snuck an extra cupcake at a birthday party? Probably. Everyone cheated. A little.

Van looked at her and felt a strange kind of calm settle over him. None of it mattered right now. Not Jack. Not Bobby. Not the glasses.

He just wanted to sit there beside her for as long as the world would let him. Right in the middle of this ridiculous, swirling, peppermint-scented chaos. Because when else would he get to sit and watch elves dance on Christmas Eve?

Van let out a soft chuckle. He wasn't sure what was funny. Maybe everything. Maybe nothing. But it slipped out anyway.

Charli felt it.

A second later, her shoulders began to shake. And then they were laughing. The kind of laugh that comes when you've cried too much. They sat there, shoulder to shoulder, laughing at the madness.

At the puppets. At the nutcrackers. At the fact that they were on trial in some weird snow-globe courtroom surrounded by dancing elves. At everything that had led them here.

They didn't stop to ask if it was real. Didn't question whether it was all a dream, or some magical illusion conjured by enchanted glasses.

This was amazing. Perfect.

And then, without warning, the floor cracked. It slithered silently beneath their legs, slipping under the table like a silver snake. It climbed the puppet judge's bench like it knew exactly where it was going.

No thunder. No creak of splitting stone. No slow, cinematic build.

Just one sharp moment. And then the floor disappeared.

Like someone had pulled the rug off the world.

Gone.

Van and Charli dropped straight down, along with a few hundred elves, a dozen nutcrackers, and an orange octopus that no one remembered inviting. They plunged into icy blackness.

The Arctic Ocean rose to meet them. Cold and instant.

The laughter cut off. Replaced by the roar of water and the sudden, shattering silence of falling.

8

Van didn't inhale the frigid, salty water of the Arctic Ocean that had swallowed him whole. That numbed him all at once.

The last thing he remembered was Charli clutching his arm. He'd grabbed her back as they plunged into the dark. But now, what he held was air. A long, fresh breath filled his lungs. He fell backward, his head sinking into the soft cushion of a crunchy bean bag.

Blackness stretched above him, wide and still, as if the world itself had been switched off.

Voices swirled around, distant and warped, coming and going like a radio struggling for signal. The floor beneath him rolled like the deck of a ship adrift on restless waves. Even his own body felt fuzzy. Like the edges weren't quite solid. Like his skin was dissolving into mist.

His lips tingled. His fingertips prickled with returning sensation. Every nerve humming.

"Hey. Hey, are you okay?"

A voice. Closer now. Hands on his shoulders. A whisper trying to cut through the fog.

Van's lips felt strangely swollen. His cheeks rubbery. His tongue a balloon filling in his mouth. A groan slipped from his throat, dry and hoarse.

He turned his head. The Styrofoam beads crunched and shifted beneath him with a sound that was both too loud and impossibly far away. It felt like he'd been asleep for days, floating through a dream that wouldn't let go. But sensation was trickling back, slow and sharp.

He forced himself up onto one elbow. That's when the glasses slipped off his face.

The moment they hit the floor, light detonated behind his eyes. Not a flash. An eruption. Blinding and white-hot, like someone had flipped the sun on inside his skull. He clamped his hands over his eyes and curled forward, trying to block it out.

When he dared a peek through his fingers, he saw the glasses on the floor. The black lenses. The faint etching on the inside.

And suddenly, everything that had happened before, every impossible thing felt real again.

"Charli," someone said through the haze. "Wake up, Charli."

Van blinked through the fuzz to find Sera kneeling beside Charli, gripping her shoulders with rising panic. Her face was pale. Tight with fear. The other girls looked just as scared. Jace too.

"I think we need to get her mom," Sera said.

Jace shook his head. "Her dad. He'll know what to do."

The others murmured agreement. Whatever they'd been laughing at when Van first came to wasn't funny anymore.

Van's mind reeled. At first, he didn't even recognize the room. It looked like someone had dumped a thrift store into a teenager's basement: mismatched bean bags, LED lights strung like spiderwebs, snack wrappers, old posters curling at the corners. For a few disorienting seconds, he was sure he'd never seen any of it before. Or the people in it.

Then, like headlights cutting through fog, recognition came creeping back. They were from school. He was in Charli's basement.

But why am I here?

And then he saw her. And it all came rushing back. The glasses.

The moment they'd slipped them on. The hat in his pocket. And that other world. The impossible one.

Was that all just a dream?

He tried to sit up straighter. His limbs trembled like he'd just finished running. His throat felt like sandpaper.

"How long…" He winced at how raw his throat was. "How long have we been asleep?"

They looked at each other like he'd spoken in some ancient, forgotten tongue.

"You just put them on," Teresa said.

"Like five seconds ago," Erica added.

Five seconds? No. That couldn't be.

He could still taste salt. Still feel the cold water in his bones. Still hear the echo of Charli's laugh from somewhere far beyond this room.

But here he was. Here they all were.

"Wait," Van said.

Jack had jumped to his feet and made for the door. He stopped with his hand on the knob. "She's not waking up."

Van lifted his hand, palm up, a quiet plea for patience. Then he crawled across the scattered bean bags and crinkled snack wrappers, over to where Charli lay. Sera had already slipped the glasses off Charli's face. They sat on the carpet beside her like a crime scene artifact.

Charli's hair was wild, a tangle of static. Her expression was eerily peaceful.

For a moment, it felt like a fairy tale. Like the kind you grow out of but never forget. Prince Charming kneeling beside the sleeping girl, not to kiss her awake, but simply to be there when she returned.

The others watched. Van tilted his head and brought his ear close to her lips. He hesitated for just a moment, then reached down and slid his hand into hers.

And that was when her eyes opened.

Charli's gaze wandered, slow and glassy. Her eyes didn't settle on anyone. Didn't blink. Didn't see. She looked like she was still there. Not here. Still drifting in whatever in-between place had held her.

Van sat back. He didn't know what she was remembering. If she saw the elves. If she remembered King Chocolate's sugar-throne, or the Sandman's voice, or the trial in the Court of Naughty and Nice.

He waited for her to remember everything. That would be okay, if she did. Just be honest, Merry had told him.

Her friends pulled her to her feet. Arms around her shoulders. Supporting her. She wobbled, knees bending just enough to make everyone gasp. But she didn't fall.

The excitement of her waking was already giving way to unease. There was something off about the way she moved. The way she didn't respond. She wasn't fully here.

Van wasn't worried. He understood.

His own mind still felt like a snow globe someone had shaken way too hard. Images and thoughts and memories swirled and smashed into each other like ornaments in a storm. He felt the floor. He knew where he was. And she'd get there too.

"We have to tell her dad," Sera said.

"What? You got to be kidding!" Erica snapped.

"Look at her!" Sera shot back.

They glared at each other, voices rising, fear sharpening every word. Charli still hadn't looked at anyone. She kept scanning the room like she was searching for something that wasn't there.

A doorway. A shadow. *A hat.*

"Let's take her for a walk," Erica said. "Get the blood pumping. That helps, right?"

The others nodded in agreement.

Three of them took hold of Charli. Erica on one side, Teresa on the other, Sera trailing behind with a steadying hand on her back. Jace crept ahead, peering down the hallway.

Farther down to the left, the Christmas party still blared like nothing had happened. Music pumped. Lights flashed red and green. The scent of sugar cookies and peppermint drifted faintly through the air.

Jace turned back and gave a quick wave. Coast clear. They moved fast. Quiet, but fast. Van rose to follow.

"Where are you going?" Sera snapped. "Haven't you done enough?"

He hadn't expected that. He didn't understand the anger. Not fully. But maybe he didn't have to. Maybe she was right. He didn't belong here. Not with them.

"She'll be okay."

"You better hope she is."

Van smirked. Just a little. Not out of arrogance. Not to provoke her. He wasn't even sure why it happened. It just did. Because somehow, it all felt right.

It was supposed to feel like this. Like he wasn't meant to stay. Like he had already seen too much.

And maybe that little smirk wasn't for Sera at all. Maybe it was for himself. A quiet, knowing grin. A reminder that he wasn't part of this world.

They guided Charli toward the door. Her steps were heavy, unsure. Her eyes didn't lift until they reached the threshold. Just before they turned right, away from the music, away from the laughter and the shimmer of tinsel, Charli glanced back.

Her gaze found Van. And for just a second, she smiled.

Then she was gone. Gone with the others, led away down the hall for a walk that might bring her back to herself.

Van let out a slow breath and dropped into one of the giant bean bags, the crunch of Styrofoam filling the silence she left behind. He stared at the ceiling, eyes unfocused.

Still smiling.

"WHERE IS EVERYONE?"

Pete popped his head into the room, his eyes scanning the emptiness before landing on Van, stretched out on the bean bag with his eyes closed.

"I think they went down the hall for something," Van said without moving.

"Everything alright?"

"Yeah." The word felt like it came from someplace deeper than just his lungs. It settled in his chest like truth. "Everything's pretty good."

"All right." Pete leaned casually against the doorframe, arms crossed. "Anyway, Lenny's getting a little anxious with the other dogs."

"Not playing nice?"

"You know how he is." Pete chuckled. "And your mom still needs to stick around and talk to some people. Do you want to take him home?"

Van was already nodding before Pete finished the sentence. He was ready. Not in the way he used to be, ready to escape, to disappear, to avoid every interaction like it came with a cost.

This was different. He just... felt done. Complete.

Like something inside him had clicked into place.

He pushed himself up from the bean bag. No wobble. Just solid ground under his feet.

"You want to say goodbye to your friends?" Pete asked, gesturing down the hallway.

Van stepped into the hallway and looked. Charli was down there. Still surrounded by her friends, still wrapped in their warmth. But now she stood a little taller. Her hands moved as she spoke, animated and alive. Her voice drifted toward them in fragments. The others leaned in close, clinging to every word.

Then she saw him. And waved.

Van raised his hand. Then he turned to Pete. "Nah. I'll see them at school."

"Good, good," Pete said, nodding. "What were you guys doing anyway?"

"We were just... playing a game."

"Oh yeah? What game?"

Van glanced down the hall one last time. "It's kind of hard to explain."

9

Christmas had come and gone, but this year, it had felt different. Not because of the gifts. Not because of the lights or the music or the eggnog. For the first time in a long time, the magic had come back. Not all of it. Just enough.

Enough to make him believe again.

Enough to remind him what it used to feel like when he was little, when the world tilted on its axis every December and became something brighter, softer, more alive.

For the first time in years, he actually liked how his mom still signed the tags "From Santa" in her curly handwriting. And when he unwrapped Santa's gifts, he didn't roll his eyes or make a sarcastic comment. He let himself believe. Just for a second.

He pictured a jolly old man standing in their living room, cheeks red from the cold, boots dripping melted snow onto the rug, sipping lukewarm milk and munching the half-broken cookies left on a chipped plate. Not Pete, scarfing them down once Van had gone to bed to keep the tradition alive.

The week after Christmas moved in slow motion. No alarms. No agendas. Just long mornings and lazy afternoons.

Van spent most of it with his mom and Pete. Together, in the same space, like something unspoken had been stitched back into place.

They played cards at the kitchen table, the worn deck missing the jack of clubs. They watched old movies wrapped in blankets in front of the fireplace, the flames crackling.

One afternoon, Van curled up on the couch beside his mom. She had a book in her hands. So did he. They didn't speak. Just read. Quiet and warm. The world outside the windows was cold and still. At one point, she nudged him gently with her foot.

"I really love this," she said.

And to his surprise, he realized something. He really did too.

VAN THOUGHT a lot about what had happened inside those virtual glasses Charli's dad had been hiding. He didn't talk about it. Not to Pete. Not to his mom. Not to anyone.

It haunted the edges of his thoughts, not in a scary way, but like a dream you keep returning to. One that doesn't fade no matter how many times you blink.

He couldn't explain how they'd lived what felt like days in that surreal, snow-globe world full of elves and nutcrackers and strange trials, when only a few seconds had passed in the real world.

Time had bent. Reality had cracked. And through that crack, something had slipped into him. Something he couldn't name.

Had Charli experienced the same thing?

She hadn't said anything. Neither had her friends. No texts. No posts. No cryptic memes that hinted at what happened inside that impossible realm.

If something had really gone wrong, he figured he would have heard about it by now.

Still, he thought about Charli. A lot. About the way her eyes had locked onto his just before she vanished down the hallway. About the faint smile she gave him. Like she knew.

And whatever that world was, virtual, magical, make-believe, it stayed with him. It had left a mark. Not a scar. Something softer. It felt like the weight he'd been dragging for months, maybe years, had quietly unhooked itself from his shoulders.

He didn't know why. Only that he felt lighter. More himself. As if that strange journey had returned something he'd forgotten. Some part of him that still believed in impossible things. In second chances. In magic.

Or maybe... it was just the Christmas spirit.

He stayed off social media, letting the silence stretch. Not because he was hiding. Because, for once, he didn't need the noise. And no one reached out. Not until Christmas break was almost over.

Then, one quiet evening, as he was sitting on the porch with a blanket wrapped around his shoulders and a mug of peppermint cocoa cooling beside him, his phone buzzed. A single text.

From *her*.

VAN NIBBLED on a slice of banana bread, trying and mostly failing not to eat the whole thing in one go. He broke off another piece and chewed slowly, trying to make it last.

The coffee was easy to resist. Still wasn't his thing.

"It's not the taste," Pete would say. "It's the way it makes me *feel*."

The café was packed, buzzing with conversation and the clatter of cups. The hiss of steaming milk, the low hum of music, laughter from a corner table. Outside, Christmas was over, but the mechanical elves in the display window kept moving, their tiny arms swinging toy-sized tools over a bed of fake cotton snow. The illusion of holiday cheer lingered, even as real life edged back in.

The bell above the door jingled as another customer walked in. That harmless, cheerful sound sliced through his nerves. He didn't think he would ever hear a little bell the same way again.

His hand twitched, itching to check the pocket of his cargo pants, just to make sure there wasn't a hat inside. Of course there wasn't. But the phantom presence was always with him now. That ridiculous, powerful, impossible hat.

Charli paused near the door, scanning the café. Her eyes landed on him, and for a second, she didn't move.

She recognized the table. *Their* table. Only, it wasn't. Because the last time they had been there... they hadn't really been there at all.

That memory was strange. Tangled. It pulled at his mind like a dream he wasn't ready to wake from. How the virtual world had captured the details of this place so precisely. Every sound, every smell, every flicker of light. Was it built from Charli's memory? It had to be. Van had never stepped foot in this café before then.

And yet, sitting here, looking around... he could not tell the difference. The polished wood of the table. The warmth of the overhead lights. The soft curve of the windows that looked out onto the snow-dusted street.

It was identical. Would he always doubt whether he was awake? He swallowed hard and pushed the thought away.

Van raised his arm and gave a small wave. She pointed at the counter, mouthing something about getting a drink. Van pointed to the empty seat and lifted the extra cup of coffee he'd ordered. Her cappuccino. Just the way she liked it. Her face lit up and hit him like a wave of sunlight.

She started walking toward him, and he couldn't help but glance around. Half-expecting to see a short, chubby man watching from across the room. Not this time. He almost wished he *was* there.

"A cappuccino with two shots of espresso," Van said, holding out the cup.

"How did you know?"

He shrugged. "I might have dreamed it."

She took the cup, sipped, and closed her eyes. For a second, she looked completely at peace. Van watched her, caught off guard by how something so small, just her, enjoying coffee could feel so right.

"So. How you doing?"

Charli opened her eyes and nodded thoughtfully, like she had to check in with herself before answering. "I'm doing really, *really* good."

Van knew exactly what she meant. He popped another piece of banana bread in his mouth.

"I told my dad about the glasses," she said.

"You did?"

"Yeah. I mean, I didn't at first, but it was like... the day after Christmas, and it just seemed like the right thing to do. I felt like I do now. Really good. I thought it was best to just tell him."

"How'd it go?"

"Oh, not great at first," she said, laughing. "It kind of ruined the whole secret hiding place thing for me. He'll probably put all his stuff somewhere else now. Or not bring them home at all anymore."

She paused, her fingers tracing the rim of her coffee cup. Then added, "But he was mostly just concerned. He said the glasses were prototypes. They really shouldn't have been used. He was surprised they even worked."

"He hadn't used them himself?"

"No, I don't think so. It sounds like they only use them in really controlled conditions back at the lab. I'm not even sure why he had them at home."

She took a breath, glancing down at the foam art in her cup.

"Anyway, he's having me go through a bunch of testing now. Something about *reality confusion.* Apparently, they're worried the glasses are so realistic, you might not be able to tell what's real and what's not after using them."

"Imagine that."

They both laughed, and the sound lingered. But beneath the laughter was something unspoken. Because she had a point. If that world hadn't been so surreal, so completely impossible, he wasn't sure he'd be sitting here now, confident this was the real world. Even now, surrounded by people and clinking mugs, Van felt slightly off-kilter.

He glanced toward the counter. The same older woman was running the café. Wiping tables, humming to herself. Just like she had in the simulation.

Except... *this is real. Right?*

"Did he say how the glasses work?"

"My dad? Oh, no. He doesn't know how most of those things work," she said, shaking her head. "He's more into managing people, handling marketing, stuff like that. I'm not even sure what he does, honestly. I know he's not an engineer, or whatever they call engineers there. Imagineers? Dream techs? I don't know. I just know he has no idea how any of it works."

Van chuckled quietly, remembering what the Sandman had said. *Do you know how a phone works?*

"He's going to tell your mom about it," Charli said. "He thinks you need to do the testing, too."

"I figured he would."

"Will that get you in trouble?"

Van shrugged. "Probably."

But his voice carried no real concern. His mom might get upset, sure. But not in a punishing way. She'd worry more about what could've happened to him than the fact that it had.

They sat for a while in silence, the conversation drifting like steam off a mug. They nibbled on banana bread and listened to the café around them. Dishes clinking. Doors opening. Laughter rising and falling like ocean waves. The cheerful old lady with the dish towel over her shoulder was wiping down tables one by one, humming a tune that sounded vaguely familiar.

"I'm sorry I didn't reach out to you sooner," Charli said.

"It's all right."

"I didn't like the way things ended after it was over, you know?" She glanced toward the window. "I'm not even sure I like my friends that much."

"Oh?"

Van wasn't sure where the conversation was heading, but he felt like it was important. Not casual important. Deep-down important. The kind of thing people say when they're finally being honest with themselves.

"Yeah, I don't know. I just feel different after we did that. But not in a bad way, you know? I'm just not really sure how I feel about them. Actually, I'm not sure how I feel about a lot of things."

"I know what you mean."

"You do?"

"I'm not sure I like your friends either."

They both laughed. It wasn't just the laughter that felt warm. It wasn't the shared banana bread or the weirdness of talking about virtual elves and dream-labs. It was something else. The stillness between the words. The way the silence didn't feel awkward. It felt safe.

That was the part that surprised Van the most.

He didn't feel awkward around her. Not anymore. Maybe it was the connection they'd shared during that impossible journey. Or maybe it was something simpler. Something more real. A bond made not from shared trauma, but from trust.

He didn't feel like he had to stare at her, searching for the right thing to say or hoping she felt something back. He didn't feel like he had to prove anything.

"I want to pay Bobby back for what I did to his tire," he said.

"You don't have to do that."

"I know. But I want to. I just don't know if I want him to know it was me. I mean, I kind of like having all my teeth in my mouth, you know?"

"Yeah, I wouldn't recommend telling him. I mean, I don't think Bobby would do anything, but some of his friends... they're a little much."

In high school, there were rules, unspoken rules that even when you did the right thing, it didn't go over well. Especially when it made someone like Bobby look dumb. Or worse. Weak. You couldn't just leave an apology note and expect it to end there.

Hey, sorry I flattened your tire. We cool? Yeah, no. That wouldn't fly.

He sighed, and for a moment, they both watched the old woman behind the counter clean a coffee spill with exaggerated, practiced grace. Charli cradled her cup again, staring down into the swirling remnants of foam. Then she looked up, her expression shifting. Something more serious.

"It didn't really happen, right?"

"No," he said. "It didn't happen."

He hesitated just slightly, the words feeling strange. Like they weren't convinced.

"I know. It's just... it's sticking with me, though, you know? Like, I can still kind of feel what that room of ice felt like. And all those elves. I can hear their voices. Smell that weird peppermint air." She paused. "It's so strange, remembering that."

Her voice lowered.

"And I... I know this is going to sound crazy, but I sort of believe it was real. You know? Not everything. Like, I don't think there are actual elves living inside the ice at the North Pole, but... I don't know what I'm trying to say."

Van didn't say anything. Because he knew exactly what she meant. He'd been thinking the same thing ever since they came back. It wasn't just some silly longing for wonder or leftover holiday hope. A part of him really wanted to believe.

"My brain says no," he said. "There's no Santa Claus. Reindeer can't fly. And even if they could, there's no way they'd make it around the world in one night. Seven billion presents? Come on. That part of my brain just says Santa Claus is for kids. It was fun while we believed, but... I mean, I can't explain what happened to us in those glasses, either. Still, I've seen magicians do card tricks I can't explain. Doesn't mean it's magic."

Charli didn't say anything, but her fingers tapped lightly against the side of her cup. She glanced behind Van. They were both thinking it. Both wondering the same thing. If they pulled aside that curtain and peeked into the pantry... would there be a present waiting on the floor?

"So," she said, "you don't believe?"

Van opened his mouth to answer. Then paused. Shrugged. He didn't want to ruin it. Not for her. Not for himself.

"You know, I was almost a queen," she said.

Van nearly choked on his banana bread. "That king would've been pretty lucky. You, not so much."

"I'll be honest, I wasn't crazy about the castle. I kind of imagined castles being... I don't know, less terrifying?"

"I was going to say creepy, but yeah, that too."

"I kind of wish I'd eaten some of that chocolate though. He did say it was the best ever, and now we'll never know."

"Yeah, I'm kind of glad we didn't. Would've probably turned us into chocolate gargoyles or something."

They started reminiscing, bit by bit, one strange memory leading to another. Like the way Ollie the octopus kept saying he was from ToyWorld. And those snowmen at the North Pole, the giant ones, with arms like cranes. They'd helped the elves haul sleigh parts and crates like it was nothing. And then there was that reindeer who had landed in the field while they were sitting by the window.

"What was his name again?" Van asked.

They both went quiet, sifting through their overlapping memories.

"Ronin," Charli said.

"Ronin! The one with the antlers like old branches."

Then Van brought up the trial. The so-called Trial of Naughty and Nice. Even now, he cringed thinking about it. That ridiculous, crooked courtroom. Sitting on the witness stand while the blue elf read off the worst things he'd ever done like they were etched into some permanent record. And Charli had been right there.

For a while, he'd tried to forget that part. Tried to file it away under *It Was Just a Dream*. But in a weird way... he was glad it had happened.

She knew now. And she didn't seem to judge him for it. What he did was pretty stupid and juvenile. He couldn't explain what came over him. But he didn't have to. Things like that happened to her too.

"Those were real-life nutcrackers," Charli said. "Like, actual nutcrackers. The way they marched and creaked when they moved."

"Yeah, but what about the blue elf? Was that supposed to be Jack Frost?"

"I guess. I just never pictured Jack Frost as, I don't know... so mean?"

"More like a villain in a musical."

"A really weird one."

"Yeah, he definitely had that vibe."

They laughed some more, remembering Jack who hadn't just been scrappy and smug, but oddly charming in a psychotic way. The kind of character who made you laugh after you realized he'd insulted you.

"The Sandman!" Charli suddenly blurted.

The people at the next table turned, startled. She lowered her voice, leaning closer. "Oh my God," she whispered. "I almost forgot. He didn't want us to forget him."

The Sandman with the gritty voice, the twinkle in his sand dollar eyes.

They kept talking, chasing one memory into another. Some details they remembered clearly. Others they puzzled over like half-forgotten dreams. The banana bread disappeared crumb by crumb. Charli drained her coffee and eventually went back for another. When that cup was gone too, they kept talking. Hours seemed to pass unnoticed.

At one point, one of the older women behind the counter, the same woman Van remembered from their first visit, or at least the one inside the glasses, approached their table with the dish rag slung over her shoulder. She gathered their empty plates and cups, wiping the table with the same smooth, practiced motion.

"You are having merry time, you two," she said with a thick accent. Exactly like before.

That voice. That rhythm. It echoed in his memory too perfectly.

"Merry, merry, Ms. Kovalchuk," Charli said. "This is Van."

"Hello there, Mr. Van." Ms. Kovalchuk extended her hand. "Nice to meet you. You have not been here for coffee yet?"

"Not really."

"Not really?" She raised a thick eyebrow. "I do not know what this means, not really. You are here, or you are not here."

"Oh, I think he means I've told him so much about this place that he feels like he's been here before."

"Ah, okay," Ms. Kovalchuk said, unconvinced. She tossed the dish rag back over her shoulder. "I don't think that's right but okay. You take care of this young lady. She is very nice."

Nice. That word would never mean the same again. "We're just friends," Van said.

Ms. Kovalchuk grunted softly, like she didn't quite believe it. But she didn't argue.

And she wasn't wrong. But she wasn't right either. Because Van and Charli were just friends. And maybe not even that, not exactly. What they had wasn't something easily labeled. It was something stranger. Something *in-between.*

As time passed, the memories of what they'd seen and done in that other world began to fade, like all dreams do. The sharp edges dulled. The impossible softened. They saw less of each other. They didn't text much. Didn't hang out. Life moved on.

But Van kept coming back to the café. He got to know the Kovalchuk sisters more with each visit. Learned how Ms. Kovalchuk made the banana bread fresh every morning, and how her sister insisted on decorating the display window with the same mechanical elves every single December.

Occasionally, he saw Charli there. She wasn't with her old friends much anymore. Especially after high school ended.

Sometimes she sat alone, typing on her laptop or reading a paperback with cracked edges. Now and then, Van would stop by her table. Say hi. They'd exchange a few polite words. Then she'd go back to her book, and he'd return to his table, sipping coffee and watching the world go by.

Every Christmas, Van made it a point to visit the café. He'd sit by the window and watch the elves moving in their little loop, tiny arms swinging, toy tools clinking, their smiles painted in place year after year.

Eventually, it wasn't the memory or the magic that brought him back. It was the coffee. And the banana bread. But mostly, it was the feeling.

That maybe, just maybe, something had been real.

Ms. Kovalchuk knocked gently on the table. "Merry, merry," she said.

Then she moved on, chatting with a nearby customer, her words rolling out in that thick, broken accent that clung to every syllable like snow to a windowpane.

"That was weird," he said. "She said *merry, merry.*"

"Yeah, she always says that."

"But that's what the elves were saying," Van whispered, leaning in across the table. "You know... inside the glasses."

"What are you whispering?" she whispered back, amused.

He shook his head. There was probably a simple explanation. There always was.

Just like there was probably an explanation for all the other little details about this café that had somehow been inside that virtual world. The green tile on the floor. The way the lights flickered when the espresso machine kicked on. The mechanical elves in the window with their never-tiring arms.

Maybe the words *merry, merry* had just filtered into Charli's subconscious, picked up from Ms. Kovalchuk and passed into the simulation like dust on a boot. Just one more echo folded into that surreal dream.

That was probably it.

OUTSIDE ON THE SIDEWALK, they shook hands. It was awkward. Too formal. They both laughed at the stiffness of it. A hug would've been weird too. A high five, maybe.

"I'll see you in class," Charli said.

"Yeah. I'll see you."

Back in class, she would always make a point to wave at him. Say hi. It felt more like a shared secret than a greeting. Van no longer found himself staring at her like he used to. He didn't twist himself up with questions about how to impress her, or what to say.

When people asked him what he got for Christmas that year, he never quite knew what to say. He'd unwrapped things, sure. Clothes. Books. A few gift cards. But none of it felt like it mattered. Because this feeling inside him, this quiet confidence, this groundedness, this peace was the real gift. It wasn't what he'd *wanted*. But it was exactly what he *needed*.

After they parted ways, Van got into his car. He started it, the engine rumbling to life, and before shifting into drive, he reached under the seat. Just to check. There was nothing there.

He would probably never see an elf hat again, not like the one from the glasses. But he hadn't forgotten the feel of it. The soft fabric. The deep, pine-needle green. The jingle of the tiny bell when it moved.

On the drive home, he stopped at a red light. As he waited, he glanced to the side. A short, bearded man stood at the crosswalk. He had a heavy coat. Round frame. His boots, if he was wearing any, were buried in a drift of slushy snow. It was hard to make out his features through the frosted window, but the man was staring directly at him.

They held each other's gaze. A horn blared from behind, snapping Van back into the present. He looked away, then checked his rearview mirror. The man was still there.

Moments like that always left a sliver of doubt. Just enough to make him wonder. Those times when the air shimmered with the scent of peppermint. When he felt, without knowing why, that someone was watching. When the line between *naughty* and *nice* didn't seem so simple.

Van never declared whether he believed in magic. Belief didn't make something real. And not believing didn't make it unreal.

But there was one thing Van held onto, even as the years passed, even as the memory softened and the world moved on. He believed in the promise of *Christmas spirit*.

That, he was sure, was totally real.

10

THE CLAUS UNIVESE SERIES

G et the 12-book holiday adventure.

Ebooks, physical and audiobooks: BERTAUSKI.COM

WELL, that's it.

This has been a prequel to *The Claus Universe*, a small story with a wide reach. If you've read the series, you may have recognized certain threads: a hat that hums with memory, nutcrackers, a reindeer named Ronin, or a snowman built from more than just snow. Each detail, each character, each whisper of magic is a breadcrumb—some obvious, some hidden—scattered across the twelve books.

If you're new to this world, welcome. If you're returning, welcome back.

All twelve books are available as ebooks through Kindle Unlimited, and you'll find paperback, hardcover, and large print editions at all major book retailers. Whether you hold the stories in your hand or read them on a screen, I hope they feel just as real as the world Van glimpsed through the glasses.

Each novel stands on its own. You can start anywhere. Dive in wherever the cover or title or character calls to you. Still, many readers tell me there's a special kind of magic in reading them in order, the way themes ripple across stories, the way faces reappear in new lights, the way the universe folds in on itself, just a little tighter each time.

There may be more books in the future. But for now, there are twelve. And if you make it through them all, you'll understand why. The twelfth book felt like the right place to stop. Or maybe... to pause. You never know with magic.

I've heard it said that time heals all wounds. But I think it's something more. Time heals when we remember. When we carry the spirit forward, year after year.

Merry, merry.

Ebooks, physical and audiobooks: BERTAUSKI.COM

The Claus Universe
12-Book Series

1. Claus: Legend of the Fat Man
2. Jack: The Tale of Frost
3. Flury: Journey of a Snowman
4. Humbug: The Unwinding of Ebenezer Scrooge
5. Claus: Rise of the Miser
6. Ronin: The Last Reindeer
7. Toyland: The Legacy of Wallace Noel